A PILGRIM'S

LAST HURRAH

DOUG MCPHILLIPS

Also, by Doug McPhillips:
Other Visionary Stories:
NOVELS.
From Darkness to Light.
Awakened to my Gutted Dream.
The Sword of Discernment.
Santiago Traveller.
I Prophet.
Master's at my table.
The Guru of Jerusalem.
We are upside down. (Biography)
The Wicklow Way.
The Adventures of Ace McDice.
Instant Karma & Grace.
The Credo.
Reflections of an Old Man.
Reincarnation of the Assassin
Masters of Introspection.
Journey to a hermit's haven.
The Rise and Rise of a 4th Reich
Grandad's tales are tall and true.
Into Action: Alcoholics for Jesus
Lightbulb Moments
For Pete's sake
Walking in My Shadow
A Camino Guide Book.
Country Camino. (Album).
Santiago Traveller. (Album).
Soul Fact. (Album).

Doug McPhillips Circa 2025 ISBN 978-1-763-8868-9-9
National Library of Australia Catalogue-in-Publication data: New Holy Bible, International Version, Hodder & Stoughton, 1980. Alcoholics Anonymous, 4th Edition, AA World Service, 1976.
As Bill sees it, 8th Print, AA World Service. 2017
Daily Reflections, 11th Print, AA World Service 2014.
Journey to the Inner Mountain, Hodder & Staughton, 2002.
The Choice is always ours, Jove Publishing, 1997.
The Sword of Discernment, Ingram Spark. Doug McPhillips 2014
Santiago traveller, Ingram Spark, Doug McPhillips, 2018.
Lightbulb Moments, Ingram Spark, Doug McPhillips, 2025
Chopping Wood, Short Run Press, David Bernz, 2023
The Times and Times of Bob Dylan: A Biography. Lulu Press, 2016.
Woody Guthrie- A Life- Joe Klein, Random House, 1999
The Mythical Journey Simon & Schuster, 1999
Notebook Research.
Google research- Authors Unknown.

" I see an intrepid adventurer plodding blindly
   through a world of booby traps, goblins and dragons."

- Author Unknown.

Content.

Introduction:

According to Buddhist tradition, the newborn Buddha took seven steps immediately after his birth. Lotus flowers are said to have appeared with each step, and with one hand pointing to the heavens and the other to the earth, he declared his final existence in this world. "Above heaven, under heaven, I am the Most Honoured One"

According to legend, the Buddha's first step was to look towards the East, where the sun rises, symbolising the light of wisdom that brings enlightenment to sentient beings, just as the sun brings light to the world. Then, in His second step, he looked towards the South. It was a display of his intention to let sentient beings know that he was the supreme field of blessing for conscious, aware beings, and whoever made even a tiny offering to him would gain immeasurable benefits.

So it was that the Bodhisattva turned his face towards the West, revealing that it was his final body in the cycle of birth and death, explaining: "The West is the direction of rest and repose. It is here that the sun sets, symbolising the eternal resting place." Indeed, in his enlightenment, it put an end to all suffering and eradicated all defilements as well as the impurity of the mind. It was written that in his fourth step, he turned to face the North, signifying that he would attain Supreme Enlightenment in his lifetime. Thus, after years of learning and severe ascetic practices in the forests, and forty-nine days of meditation under the Bodhi tree, he attained the Supreme Enlightenment, becoming the Perfect Buddha.

Then he took the fifth step, and, looking downward, let sentient beings know that his appearance in this life was to subdue all kinds of demons. In the sixth step, the Buddha looked upwards to the heavens and revealed himself as a refuge for both divine beings and humans. He added, "Heavenly and human beings must take refuge in him because only then can we escape from the cycle of birth and death. Thus, with these six steps, he traversed the entire universe."

Then, in his seventh step, he declared himself as the Honoured One: His declaration was neither born of arrogance nor made without shame - it is entirely correct, justified, and well-deserved. He proclaimed confidently, thus letting the entire universe know that the World-Honoured One had risen, and the refuge for all beings had appeared.

As he stepped through these six lotus flowers, it signified that he had traversed the realms of hell, hungry ghosts, animals, humans, Asuras, and deities and would no longer take rebirth in any of them. He had transcended the cycle of rebirth and stood at the seventh lotus flower. While sentient beings continue to wander within this cycle, the Buddha has transcended it and is no longer confined to the Three Realms of Desire, Body, and Consciousness. He was the most honoured because no one else had stepped out of this cycle of rebirth.

The story of the Buddha is a blend of historical fact and mythical embellishment. While it's widely accepted that Siddhartha Gautama, the historical Buddha, lived and taught, much of the narrative surrounding his life, especially the miraculous and supernatural aspects, is seen more as myth than fact. It is simply a man's pursuit of enlightenment. The life of any individual recounts tales of myth, legend, and folklore. It embodies what dreams are made of: achievements documented, stories shared, and humanity's relentless quest for understanding through history, encompassing birth, destruction, and rebirth since time began.

This tale that follows blends real facts with vivid fantasy, recounting a pilgrim's lifelong quest through a retrospective view of past events and experiences. As he wanders the world searching for the riddle that drives him forward in pursuit of his true purpose—an allegory for enlightenment—the writer shares a lifelong quest to discover the secret to finding meaning in life, which ultimately proves to be fruitless. He now realises, in his later years, that he will never see an object in this world capable of solving the mystery. Enlightenment comes in the form of love for another, for nature, and for the search for the eternal soul in life—things the material world can never satisfy. It is his realisation of reaching this state of inner illumination that finally transforms his quest.

So it is with this pilgrim, who, after endless pursuits of idea and action, of wandering the great earth in search of a Holy Grail, in loving and lusting, winning and losing, climbing to mountain peaks above, exploring valley floors below, riding the wild ocean waves, and coming to terms with outrageous fortune, found it all came to nothing, a dull emptiness. It is then standing at the abyss. He comes to realise that there is but one quest to complete, that in an inner journey, he just might find his enlightenment, so like the mythology of a Buddha, a Bodhi tree to sit under and contemplate.

So this pilgrim recounts his life and hopes that, in sharing his story, he and you, the reader, might find some way of understanding to live by before the final fire in the belly turns to dying ember and is snuffed out.

CHAPTER 1.
THE EARLIEST OF THE STEPS

The older man blinked as the first light of dawn crept into his lounge room, the sun's rays spilling through the window. He sat comfortably in his lounge chair, a daily habit. After finishing his hearty breakfast, he started to ponder the words on his daily reflection page. "Character is built on the anvil of suffering." Although he no longer often wrote down quotes, he liked to analyse their meaning as was his habit. He had learnt that adversity reveals one's true priorities, showing whether one's foundation is that of a warrior overcoming life's trials or if more endurance must be forged in the fires of life's hell to build resilience strong enough to face the challenges yet to come.

He had learned through bitter experience that his self-reflection was now mainly a result of his life's journey and how well he could bounce back after many setbacks that sometimes sent him spiralling into deep depression, trauma, and anxiety. He had fought the good fight, faced the challenges that came his way, and was now more than ever on a path to a happy destiny, but to what end?

The days of his adventures were now well behind him. He had to accept that his aching limbs, slow and painful movements, and faded desire to climb another mountain or chase the golden dream of conquest—whether to gain a position of power and recognition or the noble goal of finding a new love—were now a thing of the past, lost in wild behaviour.

The brave pilgrim was learning to let go, admit defeat, and accept his shortcomings, while embracing his suffering body and stilling his mind to what once was. He was now on a different quest, an inward journey of soul-searching for a place of peace and harmony within. As is often the case with those on an inward path, stilling the mind is the hardest part. So, the pilgrim of internal reflection began doing mindful tasks, such as watering his potted plants, sweeping the floor, and emptying the rubbish into the bins. The tasks that seem minor in the grand scheme of things are beyond his four walls. Nevertheless, he found them meditative to do.

The Pilgrim, the seeker, then began reflecting on his past life and how he came to this state of being. He thought of his many travels across the known world. Like so many Avatars of old, they also wandered far and wide before learning to sit and contemplate simply. He smiled at the mythology surrounding the Buddha, as he gazed at the bust of him on his balcony, sitting cross-legged; he never seemed to move, even when illuminated. Come to think of it, he had never seen a picture or a statue of the Buddha in motion. It wasn't the same with Christ, who was always moving from place to place, wandering in the desert, and later teaching his followers, "The kingdom of heaven is within."

As a young man, this pilgrim had always sought the answer to life's riddle. Though influenced by the Christian faith, he, as a wanderer, had not yet grasped the core message of Christ's teachings. Similarly, Mohammed, some centuries later, is said to have wandered the desert too, emerging as God's messenger with the Holy book, the Qur'an, to guide followers. He was the last in a line of prophets, including Adam, Noah, Abraham,

Moses, and Jesus, who, through his guidance, founded another faith, Islam.

This old man of today, mindful of both the outer journey in life and the inner spirit, no longer felt the urge to wander far from the never-ending quest he once cherished. He started to reflect on his past and recall his earliest memories of pursuing what he once believed to be his holy grail.

As memory served him well, he recalled his earliest childhood days. He was in a playpen with some trinkets to soothe him. The voices of his mother and friends in another room, waiting for his entry, made him feel like he was on stage. The Mother Lode was encouraging him to take a few steps to the applause of his audience. The memory lingered on the action that spoke louder than words — his steps were not like those of the Buddha; there were no lotus flowers at each step. He did recall that he would experience a burst of creative ideas after much suffering, before evolving to another stage. That would come later, but for now, the old man was content to recall his feelings of being able to walk strongly and faster than most babies. The family and friends clapped and praised his performance when he took his first steps. It was his earliest understanding of what love was, as the Mother Lode knew no other way to show her love than to have him perform. It took him a lifetime of learned experience before he came to terms with his early abandonment. The Mother Lode knew no better, and the Father Lode, well, he was always absent, being out of sight and thus out of mind when it came to his son.

The child, from a very young age, learnt to walk long distances and perform impressive feats such as climbing trees, making spears, killing lizards, and collecting birds' eggs to hide in his bush cave, a Holy Grail at the time. He had many friendships and took part in contact sports like rugby and boxing, as well as competitive tennis matches and long-distance running. However, he often went off on his own, puzzled that he felt different from others and didn't mind being alone. He was always trying to work out the meaning of life—his own in particular.

Building his character came at a heavy cost, as he watched his blood brother die before he reached the age of reason. Later, before he reached his teens, his closest mate drowned while they both crossed a deep tributary river to the ocean in search of the next great adventure. These memories caused him immense pain, and his only escape was to create an alter ego to live by. It was this shadow of himself that dominated him for most of his life. He saw himself as a warrior. Time and tide made him reflect on the arrows of suffering that could pierce his heart many times before he finally accepted reality and set out in search of what he was after. The memories cause him to feel pain even in the present, and he began to reflect on the alternate routes he had traversed in search of his true self.

The reality of the religious indoctrination he faced as a child was not lost on him. While it established a moral code that was hard to deny, it also left many physical scars and troubled viewpoints in a world increasingly driven by hedonism and material desires at the expense of spiritual needs. Looking back in his later years, the pendulum of biblical indoctrination—that linear, logical view of life—has, as the Christian moral landscape matures, been challenged by a sense of spiritual freedom. At least, that was his view. He came to believe in the power of a God greater than himself and to trust in inner guidance that overruled any moral judgment to the contrary. Likely it was because his freedom of thought and action was ruled by the iron hand of religiosity at the expense of his true nature. For many years, it limited his freedom of choice in matters of faith and morals.

Still, ultimately, he rebelled, as did many of his contemporaries from those post-World War years, which were vastly changed by a more modernistic world overtaking traditionalists.

It was his grandfather on his father's side who he turned to most for love during his formative years, and he received it with great attention, stories, and myth. Such that the grand old Irishman of stoic temperament knew how to fire a young boy's imagination. For he had, in his time, been a drover, gold miner, shearer, teamster, and sheep farmer. He had a litany of tales to tell, and this old man now smiled to himself, knowing that much of his storytelling, songs, and poetic expressions had been shaped by the influence of that master of storytelling.

He was growing up in the 1960s, during his teenage years, shifting from traditional songs of the pre- and post-war era to an age of Rock 'n' Roll, fast cars, heavy drinking, changing morals around safe sex before marriage, rebellious idols on the cinema screen to admire, and a freedom that his parents' understanding previously denied him. It wasn't long before he found his own way in the world, put aside soul-searching for goodness, and became as content as one can be with the shadow side of greatness. He struggled to conform, as earning a living required sticking to old, conservative ways of life. The world was entering an age of mass production, and opportunities were plentiful for anyone willing to give it a go.

Most of his schoolmates settled into a dull nine-to-five routine. They seemed resigned to sacrificing the excitement of stepping beyond their limited lives. At least, that's how he saw it. They aimed to find a girl to settle with, provide an education for their children, fall under the influence of the nesters who wanted nothing more than to see their man overburdened by a heavy mortgage, create a home for their family, and wait for retirement. To him, it all appeared dull, lacking the spirit of adventure, and he resisted it as long as he could. Eventually, he gave in after many worldly adventures—wandering from one lover to another, from one idea to another, from one country to another-until he ran out of money. That's when he turned to machining himself for work in sales, settling down with someone he believed, at the time, was his ideal; someone truly made for him. He fantasised she would be a loving wife, caring for the four children they were destined to have. To him, it all seemed so clinical, but he saw it as a natural part of growing up. Of course, he was blind to his true self and what he was meant for in the long run. He couldn't see it then, nor for another thirty years, until finally, severe suffering was inflicted upon him. He believed that taking steps towards freedom would lead to a fountain of creative ideas, marking his first step towards his true destiny.

He often went for a walk along the beach when he had a chance or headed bush, just like he used to as a kid, exploring the constant dangers of people, animals, and predators. He was never afraid of being alone because he often felt lonely inside. That's how he saw it, nature's way for him at the time.

In this moment of reflection, the old bloke headed to a local café, sticking to his usual daily routine of having a second cuppa and a rock cake, chatting with other older blokes who had more to talk about related to the past than the future. The truth was, they were all of an age where there wasn't much future left before the grim reaper would come calling, and many of them had stories to tell about how things once were. The idea of talking about the future was probably frightening to them. He noticed that all seemed to speak of their past experiences with some level of exaggeration, himself included. The more they looked back, the better they thought they were at whatever they boasted about, whether it was physical achievements, their ability with bedding women, achieving worldly success, or accumulating great wealth. The old bloke was more inclined to tell his stories in a written book or in song. He preferred to use his imagination to entertain, share what little wisdom he had, for the good of all concerned. He intended to keep hope alive for future generations.

He realised long ago that he couldn't tolerate more than an hour or two at social gatherings. The trivial chats, lack of purpose in life, and endless complaints about their situation or some physical ailment didn't interest him, though he remained courteous and understanding. This elderly man, weighed down with pain and suffering, had learnt the lessons of a life filled with hardship and heartbreak. As he shuffled his way home, he reflected on the fact that much of his trouble was of his own making. Recalling this, he began to examine how he had come to nurture his creative ideas a decade ago, when his life turned sour. He smiled when he remembered the wise words of Christian anarchist Elbert Hubbard, who had written in a literal digest in 1907, despite his own disability, about the benefit of turning the sour lemon into something of value. "Lemons suggest sourness or difficulty in life; making lemonade is turning them into something positive or desirable,

Life handed him a lemon,
as Life sometimes does. His friends looked on in pity,
assuming he was finished. They found him later,

reclining in the shade
in peaceful contentment, drinking a glass of lemonade.

Memories floated back to what had driven him to his final recovery: how suffering and hardship paved the way for creativity, the lotus flower effect of healing from deep wounds of body, mind, and spirit. He had faced ten terrible afflictions that acted as catalysts for change. Each calamity, in its own way, would have been enough for most to break down, but at the time, he believed he had the strength to overcome them all. He had buried his feelings of loss and delusion in heavy alcohol consumption, but it only brought more pain and depression when he woke from yet another hangover. Running to another woman only caused more pain, just as much for him as for them. He poured himself into many projects, and eventually, it all became too much. From childhood, he thought the best way to get through suffering was to suppress it and move on. This worked to some extent, but the weight of the many trials and tribulations he faced in later life became overwhelming, and he had no choice but to admit himself into rehab to dry out, rest, and start the process of recovery.

The old man had learnt that recovery takes time, but it's not a race. It took him a while to learn to go with the flow, live and let live. He knew, after many years of life experience, that whatever is gone is lost forever, so it was a matter of letting go and handing over to the God of his own understanding. However, that acceptance didn't come easily. It took quite a few pilgrimages before he could come to terms with himself in that regard.

The courage and clarity to venture onto a less-travelled path for him, without fear or favour, required a constant level of deep spiritual awareness before he could make it happen. This involved overcoming fear and being willing to face the dragons' mouths of psychological healing. During his first Camino de Santiago, the dragon's mouth transformed into a lotus flower of creative ideas. He had risen from the well of despair to find a new freedom of expression in poems, songs, and imaginative ideas. He was in the process of confronting everything and recovering from the night of the soul he had faced. It also brought acceptance and understanding of his inner core, shaped by his solitary nature. It was a huge breakthrough that, over time, he learnt to accept that he was a born outsider, genetically designed to be as he was. It brought him peace and hope for what lay ahead.

He had instilled in himself a core honesty, open-mindedness, and a willingness to grow, along with a desire not to worry, acceptance, and a belief in living with whatever came his way. The old man remembered how he began to relax, allowing the coil of the wound-up spring within him to unwind slowly, let go, and trust in God without definition.

Thus, the old man reflected that it wasn't the old ways of strength, enthusiasm, leadership, and dogma that would propel him like an arrow toward a set target. Instead, it was a slow journey, one day at a time, moment by moment, using the spiritual thread of the seemingly coiled spring within to unwind, loosen, and let go, thereby achieving inner calm. He remembered on his Camino that he was learning to use no force, to let the force within take hold, allowing time to heal and grow. He knew he needed to go with the grain, like an artist working with wood eventually learns. Often in the past, he had gone against the grain, resulting in splintered wounds. Now, as he journeyed back in his mind, he recalled flowing like the inner river and letting the current carry him in open water. He understood it would be an inspiring path from then on. Once he grasped and accepted the drift of it, like putting his boat of personality on spiritual waters, all it took was a gentle movement of the rudder to stay on course.

He had come to realise that following a spiritual stream of consciousness to live life on its own terms had worked effectively for him over the past decade in his various adventures. Now, however, he was feeling the weight of old age, and the daily routine burdens him with new challenges.

The Swagman

Give me the life I love,
Let the old ways wash by me,
Keep me cool by an old gum tree,
or a fireside hearth to warm me.

Let me bed down in a cave or tent,
by a riverside to bathe me,
Such is the life for a man like me,
hot damper and tea to hale me!

Here's the heart to start anew,
Whilst the summer lingers,
warmed by autumn's leafy fall,
steeled by winter's bitter.

Give me the life I love,

and the wealth before me,
Wealth I have within my heart,
Hope my soul companion.

So let the burdens fall
where they may,
Let what will be wash by me,
Give me a blue sky above,
and a bush track before me.

Loves may come and loves may go,
Friends are my true reason,
for I seek the track ahead,
with the Southern Cross behind me.

Give me the life I love,
Let the old ways wash by me,
Keep me cool by an old gum tree,
or a fireside hearth to warm me.

Let me bed down in a cave or tent,
by a riverside to bathe me,
Such is the life for a man like me,
hot damper and tea to hale me.

So let the seasons come and go,
wherever I may wander,
warmed by love of friends anew,
With no malice to the foe,
nor to life my reason.

Blind me not to springtime swell,
nor yield to come by chance,
not the power of the chase,
Just living the bushmen's dance!

So let the burdens fall where they may,
Let what will be wash by me,
Give me a blue sky above,
and a bush track before me.

Wealth I seek not, love nor hate,
nor a star to guide me,
Just the bush track ahead,
With the Southern Cross behind me.

CHAPTER 2

PILGRIM ON THE CAMINO

The old man of many adventures remembered beyond the creative output he achieved from his many pilgrimages along the Way he had travelled over the past decade.

He had learnt through much pain and suffering that the Way for him was not just the Camino Way. It was while he lay in a rehabilitation hospital about ten years ago that the idea of his path forward was to find a middle road. He had traditionally followed a linear, logical, rational, and sequential way of living in the world, but ultimately, it all came to a grinding halt for him. He had learnt to surrender, moment to moment, into the spirit of seeking rest and peace in a God of his own understanding. It was not a God of definition but a God to trust in without definition.

He had come to believe that the way forward was through spirit and imagination. A third path, balanced and moderated by his personality, like a boat afloat on the spiritual waters of life itself. While his thinking was symbolic, it proved to be a guiding influence over time. At his spiritual core, he aimed to adjust his daily routine and go with the flow of whatever life presented him. A sense of inner truth, which he would eventually see as the universal truth.

The old man's attitude and convictions had served him well in his spiritual journeys, generating a wealth of creative ideas that led to many books and songs inspired by his travels. However, now it seems different. It was as if he had been sailing smoothly on his personality boat downstream, going with the flow. But now, he has reached the vast ocean of life, with choppy, unpredictable seas, storms, and significant dangers to his spiritual well-being, health, and mindfulness. What is his mission now, in his later years? The lifeboat of spiritual reality feels dull and uninviting at the moment, and although he recognises that, unlike him, many lost souls are struggling in the ocean, in need of guidance and rescue from treacherous waters. He reflects on how he has fallen, realising he needs to look back at the point where he changed course to emerge stronger, with a renewed hope and sense of fulfilment in old age. Where is his hope now? What is his mission to achieve?

He remembered how he had lost his way for a time, and how he had once kept the flame within him burning — a flame symbolic of life itself. He recalled it all deeply, as if it were calling to him: 'Exist, stay alive, survive.' In the stillness of body and mind, the inner flame is born. Now, he needs to repeat this to feel as if he has been reborn. Stay centred. A decision to live, a choice to live, a decision not only for himself but for others as well. It was a matter of response, not reaction. First, detach his thoughts, and then I will be free. He thought, free again to evaluate the next right step. It was a matter of detachment from all desires, from a structural God, from people, places, and things. Only then could he recognise that he could trust freely, stay with the forces, and ride the waves of emotional highs and lows again.

Recalling his last Camino from about eight years ago, he distracted himself from his gloomy state of mind by planning another pilgrimage to Santiago. Looking back, he remembered how he had laid out all his belongings for the six-week journey he was about to undertake.

Packing for an adventure was nothing new to him. It was, in fact, just a continuation of what he'd done many times before. Previously, he'd set out on adventures, especially his Camino pilgrimages, when he found himself in a similar state of helplessness. The difference was not unlike his childhood escapes into imaginary worlds, when he would retreat to the bush or take long walks alone along the seashore. Although it was a solitary childhood adventure to escape into fantasy, he recalled that he'd packed his bag for those journeys, trying to come to terms with his life. However, he couldn't turn to his parents to share his feelings because they lacked heartfelt affection, especially from his mother. He had no reason to fear them; he didn't know how to express himself. He mistakenly thought his father was the strong one, because he appeared, in a worldly sense, to be wise, and he believed he would protect him from external dangers. Now, as an old man, he understood it was natural to see his mother's abandonment of his boyhood due to her depressive mindset, and as similar to his father's retreat to workaholism as an escape from a problematic home environment.

He had felt these emotions himself while recovering from depression, anxiety, and coming to terms with his alcoholism, as well as, to a large extent, the need for more affection. Now, wanting to play his part in the world again, he realised he'd been acting as he did in his previous dream life. He had no idea why he needed to walk another Camino. Despite his past and the wisdom he believed he had gained from his journeys, none of it made sense to him. Old age had become too harsh; he saw no path and could no longer live the life he once did in such an urgent and challenging world. All routes seemed blocked. Still, he knew he had to act, to try and change the world — to live as if the connection between things and their possibilities wasn't governed by strict rules but by magic. Yes, it was the magic of it all that lifted his spirits. He believed he'd written enough books, explored his creative side more than most, and done the inner work that leads to the spiritual. But now, it felt more like an awakening — the will to trust in the magic. As he packed his essentials for another pilgrimage, he was sure that, at last, he was onto something…

He was recalling the most brilliant technique for transforming life: an impractical self-observation to "go where Saturn would lead him." The magic was upon him! To align with the astrological influence of Saturn, which is linked to discipline, responsibility, and long-term goals.

It was not the straightforward logic of the world he was now tuned into. He had been there and done that. He was ready to embrace a deeper kind of hard work, accepting his own limitations and learning from challenges, even in his creative pursuits. He now understood the importance of letting go completely. He had claimed he could, but this was different—difficult but not impossible. Essentially, he needed to navigate life's structures and responsibilities with maturity, focusing on building a solid foundation for the future. He had pushed the limits too far in his quest to find his inner holy grail. Sure, his output in writing and recording songs for others would leave a sort of legacy, but it didn't matter in the end. What was truly important now was, first and foremost, his health. He had surrendered to a Higher power and used his skills to create opportunities for himself and others, rekindle his sense of humour, be wise, control his energy, be worthy of love, and be kind. Reach out to those in greater need than himself. He knew he just had to stay calm, cool, and collected. Everything would be restored in God's good time.

He remembered how the Camino journey sparked a unique creativity in his life. The series he wrote helped him understand the world more clearly. During his pilgrimages, he uncovered many myths and legends. In ancient times, myths and folktales were used to explain natural events, such as why the sun rises, why storms happen, or what inspires bravery. These stories taught valuable lessons, passed down traditions, and kept memories alive. Even though the world looks very different now, those old stories still speak to something deep inside him. He recalled his grandfather's tales, which he had come to believe in his old age, were mainly mythological stories of his travels. It had been his way to cope with the hardships of being on the road, and he had travelled through time, sharing his experiences with the old man when he was a boy, from one culture to another.

On the Camino, he also connected with big ideas in myths: good versus evil, the hero's journey, and the struggle to find one's place in the world. His stories show that people have always grappled with the same questions: What does it mean to be brave? How do we face loss? Where do we find hope? He had long ago decided that his pilgrimages were more than just tales of myth and legend that resonated with his soul's purpose.

In his past writings, he wove Spanish mythology and folklore into his pilgrimage to the Holy Grail, creating a sense of wonder. It felt familiar, even if the setting was entirely new. His storytelling was lively and vibrant. Back then, he believed his readers felt connected to his story, to one another, and to the long line of storytellers before him. He spoke of belief in the people of the past, in magic, monsters, myth, and folklore, which served as a guiding light for those walking the Way.

They were merely stories about people's fears, hopes, mistakes, and dreams. He was like a wandering collector of stories, twisting them with his imagination into tales of love, lust, sacrifice, betrayal, injustice, and the fight to change life's path from material to spiritual in search of meaning and a new destiny. His stories reflected his own life, marking a shift from worldly values to inward ones. Overall, like his fellow pilgrims of The Way, regardless of their trials and tribulations, their journeys—whether past or present—were fundamentally human experiences.

He had set out on a quest, a mission to live differently, but during his search, he realised it was all an illusion. Maybe he had unknowingly been searching for the Holy Grail, that legendary artefact, the most renowned cup used by Jesus at the Last Supper, and later used by Joseph of Arimathea to catch his blood at the crucifixion. It may not have been so, for what would he want of his blood? This symbolism and tradition are possibly linked with the legend of later Christian belief regarding the Holy Grail and the blood of Christ, for it was Joseph who reportedly took Jesus down from the cross, wrapped him in a cloth, and buried him in his tomb.

The old pilgrim remembered linking the Arthurian legend with miraculous healing, the magic of a spiritual quest that he had misunderstood in these circumstances. He had certainly walked the path with a mission each time he went on a pilgrimage, but they all turned out to be false flags regarding his true purpose. He had overlooked the significance of St. James' journey, preaching throughout northern Spain and especially on the Iberian Peninsula.

After St. James' remains were discovered about 800 years after his death, or at least reported as such, Christian troops had already scattered ashes on the battlefield before a fight against the Moors, having taken some ashes from the tomb where he was laid. This was followed by a sighting of St. James riding a white steed, holding a flaming sword aloft and leading the troops into battle, whom they credited with their victory. This belief was strengthened by the fact that Christianity was short of funds to fight the battle, and a local bishop, upon being presented with the bones and some ashes found by an old, brave searcher, quickly confirmed they were the remains of St. James. Thus, the bones were laid beneath the altar at the Cathedral of Santiago. Since medieval times, the route St. James supposedly took on his quest to convert pagans has been trodden by pilgrims, who share the goal of shedding their burdens—be it a heavy object like a rock or an offering—or laying down their sins at the altar in Santiago's Cathedral, where the remains of the warrior apostle of Christ lie.

The old man visited the tomb three times, but it was of no real use then, as he didn't believe St. James' remains were buried there. He thought it was just another myth, like many others he'd come across in Spain, where myth and legend are still retold. In truth, in his research, he found no proof of any battle ever taking place on the Iberian Peninsula. The struggle in his quest was in a far-off province where the Moors and the Christians were fighting over territory that held valuable metals like gold, silver, and bronze. So, like all these modern-day pilgrims' approaches to life, he was a doubting Thomas — the one who said that unless he put his hand in the wound of Jesus' side and touched the hands of the crucified Christ, he would not believe that he had risen from the dead. In the same vein, to him, St.

James never set foot in Spain, but he still said a prayer at the tomb, just in case he was wrong about his assumptions.

The old man had turned to the Camino Way at that stage of his life, feeling sad and burdened by a lot of suffering. Lost in his past achievements, seeking worldly rewards, he shifted his focus inward, and the idea of a pilgrimage began to take shape in his mind. In retrospect, it seemed to him that he was born for it. Born to be reborn into a new way of living.

The first Camino pilgrimage was about shedding old burdens, like the pain of a broken marriage, the loss of a son by his own hand, and losing his means to earn a living. He hadn't planned it; instead, he simply packed his knapsack, carried a tent and a sleeping bag, and stepped into the unknown. He felt a kind of relief that he was on a new path to freedom, one he hadn't encountered before. He downloaded from a travel log where the pilgrimage started, the distances between towns, and the final destination - Santiago de Compostela. No map, no guiding light, no idea of what lay ahead. He made his way to the airport and caught the next flight to Paris, France.

On his journey, he met pilgrims of all ages, but he was particularly drawn to the young, as they were stepping out on their rite of passage to a new way of life. Though he was older, he felt he was also like them. All that he had ever lived for, done, and believed seemed to be burned away from him internally. He had chosen this path to let go of the old and embrace a new way of living. He wasn't sure what exactly, but in a quiet moment, it was suddenly revealed to him. The old man realised that, above all, he was a creator of myth and folklore when it came to his pilgrimages. The characters, the drama, the big questions—they had endured for a reason, for a season. Now, he was involved in something profound and inspiring—reworking stories that have shaped his life over the past decade. Reflecting on entire cultures and generations, he could give them a fresh spin that was uniquely his own. He saw it as a challenge, a chance to make something timeless feel new again.

The change that came over him followed more suffering. It was a fall he had in Paris before setting off on the Camino Way. It was a shift from light into darkness. He had entered the hotel foyer from the bright sunlight into a dark reception area, where he had booked for the night. He had tripped on the entry step and tumbled headfirst, thrown forward by the heavy backpack on his back, and landed on his face.

The brave adventurer was up bright and early the next morning, nursing a headache, two black eyes, and a bruised nose. He was determined not to let personal setbacks ruin his adventure. Additionally, he had decided to lift his spirits above the dull way of life he had once known, a man of many sorrows. He made his way on foot to Gare Montparnasse, a central rail hub for city travellers, to catch a train to a foreign destination called Tour de Maine-Montparnasse, the tallest structure in Paris after the Eiffel Tower. It served as a guiding beacon for the rail network, so this adventurous traveller couldn't help but find his way. He purchased a one-way ticket to St Jean Pied de Port, the ancient village on the border of France and Spain, at the foot of the Pyrenees Mountains. Soon enough, he was travelling on the fast train. After placing his backpack on the rack above his head, he settled into his seat for the six-hour journey ahead, still nursing his headache. Determined to keep his mind off how he was feeling, he began to recall the hardships and difficulties his grandfather had faced in life on the road — drover, gold miner, and teamster; he then started writing a poem about the exploits of his beloved "Pop" — the one whose stories he told as a child that fired his imagination. He didn't know then that this poem would spark a cascade of creative ideas that would flow from him over the next decade, leading to many novels and songs.

Now, in his hermit-like existence in the present, he was reflecting on the value of it all. He thought of Jesus' statement when asked where he was going. He responded, "I must go to Jerusalem." It was a biblical reference to Jesus' journey to fulfil his mission of suffering and death on the cross. Of course, his first pilgrimage to Santiago de Compostela couldn't compare, but that journey marked a transition from his previous outlook on life. Through suffering and letting go, he discovered a new spirit of adventure—an inward journey to find a way of life he could no longer turn away from.

He remembered that on his journey, he met pilgrims of all ages, but was especially drawn to the youths stepping out on their rite of passage to embrace a new way of life that he had never known until then. Although he was much older, he felt very much like them. All that he had ever lived for, done, and believed in seemed to be burned away from him internally. He had chosen this path to let go of suffering, regrets, and the life he had led. At the time, he believed it was a way to shed the old and embrace a new way of living. At first, it was revealed to him through creative output. However, he was now coming to terms with the fact that it was more than that. On that path, he met a rock and folk musician who later recorded his poem about his grandfather's life, 'boundary rider,' into a song. This was the catalyst that propelled him into war stories and songs for the next decade, but was it all in vain?

He had tramp the Way to Santiago three times in the past. Learnt to live a life on the road, not wanting for the world of material things, but had he been fooling himself? He had tramped the well-worn route of Christ's Apostle St. James, who had reportedly walked the northern route of Spain preaching the truth in the belief that Faith without works is death. Did he live according to the truth that "action speaks louder than words"? He had written many words since his first Camino, but was that the action required of him now?

As an older man, his Camino journeys were undeniably physically demanding, but more importantly, they were spiritually and emotionally healing. In an interview, he stated, "The Way is a journey of awakening and enlightenment. It taught me not to be burdened by need, nor even the desire, for the material things society often defines as signs of success in this world." He had to admit that the one thing he had not let go of in the material world was the desire for recognition. Now, in his cottage, if he received it, would he truly cherish it? Upon deep reflection, it had little to do with recognition or stroking the ego, but with his sense of abandonment. He had never really come to terms with the fact that the applause he received as a child was a false flag. Despite the many relationships he had throughout his lifetime, had he ever truly loved?

The opportunity had arisen to rework his old characters and stories he had already written into something more relevant to now. He looked at his pre-filled backpack, ready for the next adventure. Did he want to trudge over hill and dale, and was that the most worthwhile use of his time? Here he was now in the present, older, slower in his movements, still capable of adventures, but the fire within did not burn with the same intensity. He could venture out there and return to weave another story into his chapters of wandering, but he was no longer motivated to do so.

CHAPTER 3.

TRAMPING ONWARD

The Pilgrim had learned that loving someone truly is more than just a feeling; it's a state of being that involves a deep connection, respect, and a willingness to prioritise the other person's happiness and well-being over one's own. It took time to reach acceptance, forgiveness, and a desire to see his love flourish, even if it meant occasionally sacrificing his own desires. It's a journey of vulnerability, trust, and unwavering support. This is what he had dreamed of, but it never arrived until he let go of the idea that he would find true love. Then it came unexpectedly, someone who cared beyond material worth, beyond lust or any other motive, for she was there for him whenever he was in need, and she loved and respected him, as he did her.

However, he still valued his own space, his freedom, and the choice that continued to define him as a bit selfish. He had tempered his desire for independence, which often meant being alone with his thoughts and feelings, because once he set himself a task, he had to see it through.

What would change if he decided to rework his old stories into something new? He was no longer driven by fame or wealth. The desire for women had faded, as he was content just being with himself. So, what now was the core of his being? He kept the backpack ready just in case he felt inspired to head out again, but at his current state of mind, it seemed unlikely. He remembered the many myths and legends he had written about from his first Camino. Myths and folklore explore universal themes, such as love, heroism, betrayal, and destiny. He had lived many of these experiences himself and had set out on his second Camino with an idea for another story —a search for love —but in truth, he just wanted to be with a foreign beauty. Like myth and folklore, the truth was that he didn't find love, but lust, and all the sorrow that follows such artificial encounters. The 'pilgrimage', **as he saw it**, was a blind spot for his selfishness, but ultimately, the truth and his search still mattered.

He remembers how he ruined both relationships in the process. He knew he'd need to make amends eventually, but his passion and lustful behaviour had sent him back into rehab and a lengthy stay to recover from his depressed state of mind. At least this time, he was spared from falling back into the chaos of excess.

He had published a book of poems, a novel based on his Camino, and written and recorded his first album of songs before his last Camino, but he wondered if he had truly reached the depths of his creativity. He decided to walk the Camino again for the third time. It was for himself; to go cold turkey off the heavy medications he was on. The way for him to beat the withdrawal effects of drugs was to walk the Camino and venture across Ireland to do more trekking over hill and dale. He had been content to be on his own, write poems, and take copious notes for his next book- a mythical tale of a man on his third Camino, looking back on his first and second journeys and the lessons learnt. It had a mythical plot showing the hero facing enormous challenges. He remembered now that readers related to the hero being scared, yet determined, courageous, and foolhardy.

The old man wondered why he had lost his enthusiasm for life, unlike the carefree days on the Camino, his mountain hikes in Ireland, or crossing the slopes of volcanic peaks in New Zealand. It wasn't that he couldn't do it again, but he lacked the will to get out there. He was reminded of the need to be brave; that meant facing danger, fear, or hardship, summoning the strength to push forward, persevere, and take action. He himself was the one who had stepped out without fear of others' opinions on his first Camino, armed with inner strength to conquer his depression, let go of the past, and seek his inner muse for guidance. He was sixty-eight at the time. Then, just two years later, at age seventy, he was on another Camino route in Portugal, this time in search of love, discovering the power of lust and the downfall that followed. It had taken a lot of courage on his third Camino, at the age of seventy-two, after spending months in another rehab hospital, to overcome depression, for him to once more step out on another Camino adventure to reconnect with his creative muse. Many books followed that Camino, and many songs were written, sung, and recorded. So what was it now that caused his lack of enthusiasm for adventure? He decided that if he wanted to go out there, he would have to invent one.

On examination, he realised that most of his stories were rooted in myth, exploring the human condition. They include universal themes, such as love, heroism, betrayal, and fate. His myths depict a hero facing foes, fighting his creative dragon—something no one does today—yet a reader can still relate to the hero's fear, determination, and hope for the future. He knew he had the ability to start something new but understood that when using myths, he didn't need to begin from scratch. There are plenty of characters, archetypes, and plots to build upon. He was thinking of the trickster he knew, the wise mentor who, at his core, aimed to encourage him to take a different path—leading him to write his first novel—or the one who had studied someone like himself, someone who craved power only to fall on their sword. He knew that readers often recognise these types of characters, which motivates them to keep reading. So, he figured he could draw on the work he'd already done to create a familiar feeling. But he needed to be within his muse's influence to be truly original.

He considered adding fresh twists, like shifting a character's perspective or setting the story in a futuristic city, but that wasn't his initial idea. Instead, he realised he needed to reread all twenty-five of his books, highlighting the relevant passages about himself and his current state, then rework them into something original for his readers. He saw it as a worthwhile goal, and one he now wishes to pursue.

Then the thought of these stories being erased from his past, just like his Camino pilgrimages and memories of old, struck him. He knew he would need to recall other memories, which meant revisiting the chambers of darkness. He had lived through it all; now he needed to do this for the last time—to confront the dark shadows that once caused him to become depressed and anxious, though they no longer affected his present state of mind. They were just memories of those who had passed that no longer haunted him. Sometimes he woke from a dream of some disturbing event he had experienced long ago, but mostly it was a pleasant recall. He needed to be sure that whatever transpired from here on in had nothing to do with his past. So, as a brave pilgrim on an inner journey, he began walk-

ing through the graveyard of his memory, visiting the tombs of
those he had once known.

Wounded love heart.

Now my heart beats
to a drummer,
That's not quite the same as the rest,
It's where I long to be free,
attuned with the sound in my chest.

Listen to the rhythm of a heartbeat,
The sound of a different drum,
not the beat of a heart for another,
nor the weary heart wounded by love.

It won't be found in worldly values,
where money's the ultimate quest,
not the beat of a heart in battle,
where they pinned a medal
on your breast.

It may be found when in tune with nature,
where man is at one with the plan,
climbing a rugged mountain range,
tilling and planting the land.

Sailing the blue of the ocean,
viewing the flight of a bird,
hearing the sound of cicadas,
deep in a forested wood.

Catching a fish for survival,
cooking it on one's fire,
sleeping out in the open,
Watching the star-filled sky.

Seeing the sunrise at dawn,
plainly being in tune,
living the now when it's crowded,
being quite still in a room.

It's being in tune with one's senses,
The music you have in your heart,
conscious of each passing moment,
The wounded love hearts where you start.

It won't be found in worldly values,
where money is the ultimate quest,
not the beat of a heart in battle,
where they pinned a medal
on your breast.

Now I know my heart beats
to a drummer,
That's not quite the same as the rest,
It's where I long to be free,
attuned with the sound in my chest.

CHAPTER 4.

GHOSTS OF THE PAST

The old pilgrim now remembered how he used to experience visits from family members after their passing. Sometimes it was a scent, a ghostly image of their presence, or a strong feeling of being near them. Perhaps it was his mind's way of helping him cope with their loss, he thought. But he had felt all these things before, and now he saw them as memories, not as them being dead, but as they were when they were alive, just like him.

The older man's mind drifted back to a graveyard he had visited before, searching for the burial site of his best mate, who drowned when they were twelve-year-old boys. It had been about eighteen years, and now there were even more gravestones than he had imagined. Headstones revealing people from his youth lying there beneath the ground. He saw them as they once were, as large as life, just as he remembered them on a particular day. Mitt, known as Michael the Dentist, whistled on his way to work as he strolled along the main street of the little village where he was born. Mitt had always been a good bloke, seeing life with a "glass half full" attitude. Whether he was pulling a tooth or enjoying the fresh air, he always seemed happy. Now, his remains lie at the old man's feet.

He searched the heads anxiously, looking for the headstone of his boyhood mate. A headstone that would seem to stir a memory, like 'Spike,' the local hardware bloke, who sold ales in a rush but was a friendly fellow all the same. 'Bumpy,' the war hero who came back from WWII shell-shocked and took to drinking his life away. He was often seen heading home drunk from the pub on horseback, or in the middle of summer, with a bush branch in hand to brush off the flies, repeatedly saying, "There are no flies on Bumpy." Many of his mates from his youth had now passed on, and he wondered, as in biblical teachings interpreted by Solomon, which explore themes of morality, wisdom, wealth, pleasure, and the humid conditions. He pondered Solomon's purpose of it all, if it ends in death. He remembered that Solomon had finished his Ecclesiastes with, "Good food and drink in pleasant company, offering it all to God, was all that man could expect from life." He also recalled Rembrandt's constant mantra from the wisdom of Solomon, as he went about his work painting masterpieces, mumbling: "Vanity of vanities, and all is vanity."

The old man, after many visits to the headstones of people he once knew, couldn't bear it any longer. Eventually, he found his friend's gravestone and meditated over it for a while. Still, he couldn't stop crying for his losses and the reminders of gravestones that forced him to let go of memories, pray for their release from life's flaws in the spirit world, and carry on within the mystery of everything.

The memories of others from his childhood drift forward as if they are real. "Colin," the mechanic who worked for my father, with his funny sense of humour, says, "There was 'Bob', who also worked for his father, who was an authority on everything and who eventually left the mechanical world to become a life insurance salesman— a fitting job for an outlandish loudmouth. [I ought to know, I had many years in that line of work too.] Then along came Cactus," that prickly character who often took us to the beach when we were kids. He was the one who started the 'Nippers,' the children's surf lifesaving club that grew into a statewide institution for childhood beach activities. Others drifted into mind, but the old man decided to focus on more pleasant memories. His mind visualised a particular New Year's night party at his house during his boyhood. He had been allowed to stay up all night and enjoy it. Memories of a room full of partygoers, drinking, singing, and playing the piano. When it came to his father, he was always the centre of celebrations and attracted talented artist types. His father was quite different—more linear, logical, and mathematical, and brilliant as an engineer. While he played the piano himself, he preferred to be my host rather than the resident entertainer. The old man pictured "Trevor" with his baritone voice singing Old Man River while "Roy," an accomplished pianist, served as the leading musical entertainer. There had been small moments of happiness in that household, but they were few and far between, he recalled.

Looking back, none of the memories he recalled of others, including those in the graveyard, were unpleasant. It only seemed tied to his relationship with his Mother and Father that he felt this sense of sadness and abandonment, which had distressed him, and he wondered why he wasn't troubled by it all now. He told himself that, in revisiting the spirit of the past, it was his way of coming to terms with the people who appeared to shape his personality from beyond the grave.

Lately, he had many dreams centred on money—either about its absence or struggling to reconcile it in the present. Since he had lost his fear of financial independence, he wondered why he kept having so many dreams about money. He guessed that perhaps it was a form of spiritual currency existing beyond the real world of the living. He needed to look back and let go to move forward now. It was an awakening to realise that he had tapped into the intangible resources of compassion, generosity, and love, which not only enriched his life but also helped to enrich the lives of others. For he now believed that such dreams might continue until he had completely let go of the material world.

He was reminiscing about a vivid dream he had many years ago. In it, he dreamt of "The Wizard of Oz," where the Scarecrow, Tin Man, and Cowardly Lion represent the virtues of intelligence, compassion, and courage, respectively. They accompany Dorothy on her journey to Oz, each seeking these qualities from the Wizard, but ultimately realising they already possessed them. The Scarecrow symbolises a lack of intellectual capacity, yet he desires a brain, even though he demonstrates cleverness and problem-solving skills throughout the journey. The Tin Man represents the absence of a heart, yet he is compassionate and caring, showing concern for others, including animals. The Cowardly Lion signifies a lack of courage, despite his intimidating appearance, but he faces his fears and bravely confronts danger. The characters' journey with Dorothy emphasises that true fulfilment comes from recognising and embracing the virtues they already possess, rather than seeking them from an external source.

The old man in his dream embodied all of these characters. He had embraced the others except the Tin Man, who walked his way down the hill away from the two other characters, singing: "Oh! Yes, I'm that great pretender, pretending that I'm doing well..." It would be a decade after that dream when the old man reignited his mind, which had been dormant in a spiritual sense, even though he was clever in a worldly sense and good at problem-solving. The Scarecrow in him took time to use his creativity to help others. Like the Lion in the story, he had to learn to show compassion and care for others to regain his courage. The Tin Man, who could not find his heart, was the one going down the hill singing. When, in the dream, he took off his tin mask, it was himself as a man.

There seems to be great significance in this dream, as the other characters had found their way, but the Tin Man was still struggling, and the old man realised that his subconscious had been in tune with that for a long time. He had been trying to show love, and now it was right in front of him. What he was experiencing was his alter ego's realisation that he was no longer sad, lonely, or confused. It was his experiences of life as someone who had mistakenly not loved, even though he professed to, and now was learning to love. He now felt he knew something about life, something from the core of his being that he could never find in books, and it all stemmed from love.

Then there is Dorothy, who draws the child inward, seeking a way back home. He had not focused on that in his dream. It has always been his Achilles' heel to seek and find answers and a way back home, and it is the story within himself, the relationship of those characters in the tale. We might think that the world is full of evil and destruction, and that this stage may last forever, but that is not true. The old man concluded to himself that we as humans are capable of creating more evil every day, in the oceans of shattered lives, starving millions, and potential or actual wars. Still, we also have a great capacity to overcome this through our inner spirit. When one day the ignorance born of childhood repression is eradicated and humanity awakens, an end can be put to the personification of evil.

The old man enjoys exploring philosophical ideas or theories related to his current outlook. He was very aware of how much time he had spent writing books, some of which were spiritual and thought-provoking, all dealing with the meaning of life. It helped him, at least in theory, to understand the concept of life's meaninglessness, especially now that he was closer to the end than the beginning of his time on Earth.

He had, with some insight, realised that any written approach or answer to the dilemma of life and death is merely an aesthetic experience once it is written and read. The work's connection to salvation may only be temporary. Therefore, it is not a proper redemption, as it never endures. In other words, while all things might have meaning in the present, they ultimately fade away and perish, just as we ourselves must do.

He was contemplating the start of Fear in Trembling. In the section titled "Eulogy on Abraham," Kierkegaard describes the world as a cruel and malevolent primal unity to be rejected. At the same time, he portrays an orgiastic frenzy of chaos to be embraced. This might be called the aesthetic view, which, if true, would rule out any genuine recognition of individual human suffering as impossible: if a human did not possess an eternal consciousness, and if beneath everything there was only a wild, fermenting force that, writhing in dark passions, produced all things—significant or insignificant—if a vast, relentless emptiness hid beneath the surface, then what would life be but despair? If such were the case, with no sacred bond tying humanity together, if one generation arose after another like forest foliage, if generations succeeded each other like bird songs in the woods, if one moved through the world like a ship crossing the sea or wind blowing across the desert—an unthinking, unproductive performance—if an eternal oblivion, perpetually hungry, lurked for its prey, then there would be no force strong enough to tear that away. Life would be an empty, consolation-less existence.

He thought of a line from Shakespeare's Julius Caesar, when those would-be assassins met to plot the demise of their ruler; it was Cassius who, like himself, was the plotter of evil deeds. "Yonder Cassius has that lean and hungry look; he overthinks; such men are dangerous." Yes, it was true that the old man overthought it too much about the meaning of life instead of just living it, despite the constant acceptance of being alone, sometimes suffering, but with letting joy, other than to meet his fellows of similar age, who too were enduring the latter days like himself.

It was then that the mind wanderer decided to revisit his writings from the past decade, hoping that some treasure from the other side, or a paragraph he had consciously written before, would lift his spirits even more by recounting an adventure or sharing some insightful work that might help him through his current struggles of adapting to life now in his daily dotage. He was also mindful of his mission to keep his readers informed for their mutual benefit.

He reconsidered his past pretence, now reflecting on those he realised he had loved but lost because of his foolishness. He thought about the devil-may-care life he had led as a gambler, drinker, and a good-time Charlie. Back then, he had a knack for making money, being not just an alcoholic but also a workaholic. While providing financial security for himself and his loved ones, he recognised that his behaviour over the years was somewhat unpredictable, risk-taking, and in need of redemption. He concluded that he had learnt life's lessons the hard way, and now, in his older years, it was all about making amends and showing compassion for others.

Oh-oh, yes, I'm the great pretender
Pretending that I'm doing well
My need is such, I pretend too much
I'm lonely, but no one can tell.

Oh-oh, yes, I'm the great pretender
Adrift in a world of my own,
I played the game but to my real shame,
You've left me to grieve all alone.

Too real is this feeling of make-believe
Too real when I feel what my heart can't conceal
(Oh-oh-oh-oh-oh-oh-oh-oh-oh)

Yes, I'm the great pretender,
just laughin' and gay like a clown
I seem to be what I'm not; you see
I'm wearing my heart like a crown
pretending that you're still around

Too real is this feeling of make-believe
Too real when I feel what my heart can't conceal
(Oh-oh-oh-oh-oh-oh-oh-oh-oh)

CHAPTER 5.

ONE STEP BACK, TWO FORWARD

In contemplating his current state of mind, the old man realised how vital it is to accept life on its own terms. Some days would be full of joy, and he would feel healthy, lively, and active. On other days, though, when the sky was cloudy and grey or it was wet and gloomy, and his body ached with pains, he would feel despondent. In his present circumstances, he was reminiscing about a story he had read in a magazine during his first Camino that illustrates the importance of embracing suffering and joy as parts of life, regardless of the situation.

King Gougia, in the grand tale of that ancient Chinese ruler from the 5th century CE, was captured by his arch-enemy and imprisoned for three years before being granted amnesty. Instead of returning to his throne, he chose to eat peasant food and live. He slept on a bed of brushwood and tasted an animal's gall bladder every day to feel life's bitterness. It was a reminder of the shame and humiliation he endured in captivity, and he drew strength from it. The memory of that story lifted my spirits; I believed that I could, for most of the day, survive off the malnourishment I had just consumed, but I didn't think about how my energy could be maintained in the now sweltering heat if this Spanish morn.

The old man reflected on Chinese traditional medicine and how the gallbladder is linked to decision-making, courage, and judgment. It is believed to be the "official of justice" and plays a role in a person's ability to make choices and act decisively. It is also connected to emotions like anger, frustration, and irritability. Beyond its emotional and mental aspects, this traditional Chinese medicine also recognises a physical link between the gallbladder and muscles and connective tissue. In Chinese medicine, the gallbladder and liver work together, and a balance between them is essential for making decisions, planning, and feeling grounded. So, although the story here is merely a mythical tale, it serves as a reminder to the old man to accept life on its terms, the bitter with the sweet.

He had done just that on his Camino pilgrimages, as he recalled. Although he sometimes got caught up in the pleasures of the flesh, his true aim was to accept the bitter with the sweet. It took him three Camino journeys to understand the importance of letting go and going with the flow. The symbols along the way hadn't been lost on him. Whether it was the scallop shell signpost along The Way, symbolising that all roads lead to Santiago de Compostela, the place reportedly of the tomb of St. James, the Apostle of Christ. It was a journey to overcome the night of the soul, to once again dare to accept that one had to do penance to be enlightened to live, really live, renewed in spirit.

He was reflecting on the signs he had embraced along The Way. Some of those signs he remembered had a more worldly connection, yet they also held a present-day significance—about the freedom he was experiencing, and the link with living in the world but not of it was not lost on him. He recalled a long day's journey, walking 215 km from León in the heat of midsummer with an overloaded backpack, arriving at a village albergue, the Refugio de Jesús on the desert plain. It was unique, as on the walls of the Refugio, from floor to ceiling, were covered with graffiti-like quotations, some new, others almost faded, scrawled by pilgrims over many decades. A quote from Jack

Kerouac's famous nineteen-fifties novel, "On The Road", attracted him: "They danced down the street like dingledodies, and I shambled after., as I had been doing all my life, after people who interest me, because the only people who interest me are the mad ones, the ones who are mad to live, mad to talk, mad to be saved, desirous of everything at the same time, the ones that never yawn or say commonplace things, but burn, burn, burn like fabulous yellow roman candles exploding like spiders across the stars, and in the middle you see the blue centre light pop and everyone goes 'Awww!' [Dingledodies is not a standard dictionary word, but rather a term Kerouac uses to evoke a sense of wild, unrestrained joy and a love of life. It suggests a carefree, almost manic, enthusiasm for living.

While the old man could relate to Kerouac's deliberate break from the suburban, middle-class Australian dream, he and his contemporaries, known as the Beat Generation, actively challenged societal norms about work, family, and possessions. Like Kerouac, he had tried to defy the conservative life when everything went south for him. He was also searching for meaning and grappling with questions of spirituality and purpose. While Kerouac's work explored themes of religion, loss, and reality, he celebrated a life of freedom and experience in his writings. The old man realised he too had been heading down that path, like Kerouac, who succumbed to alcoholism and drug addiction, which led to his early death at 47. Somehow, life lessons pulled him back from the edge. He could thank his sobriety to the help of friends, the way he sobered up and turned to God for guidance — even if he still found it hard to define his beliefs — he knew he didn't need to drone on, but he was thankful it worked; it was comforting to know that.

A memory of his morning walk to a cafe on the Portuguese Camino came flooding back. Another sign scribbled on a wall had caught his eye.

"This is how good ideas are crazy…

that I have the maximum forms of strange facts,

unmistakable colours,

now they amaze,

Now thy shroud,

obscured as background

In a bottomless pit of my thinking ."

The old man was now questioning his own authenticity. Did writers like Jack Kerouac, Hemingway, Thomas, and Joyce stay true to themselves, or did they wear masks, caught up in a world of wild ideas? Were they honest with themselves and others, taking responsibility for their actions and making choices that truly reflect who they are? The consequences of their actions proved otherwise, as alcoholism, drug use, and the pleasures of the flesh interfered with their true natures. He was not one to judge, as he too had succumbed to the world rather than the spiritual. They, like him, had been on the search, delving deep into the meaning of life, but not into the discipline of their nature; they were sadly lacking. It was not that the old man was being too critical of those great, talented men, but rather, he was seeking answers for his soul. The lives of men of worldly renown seemed a more realistic template to measure against than those of saintly individuals who, in a religious sense, were just as famous but whose lives appeared less appealing to him.

He recalled his wandering with the youth of that time on his first Camino in 2013. He had trudged the weary path of his Camino, letting go of someone who was worn out by the world but also trying to make up for missing out on rites of passage as a young bloke. It was a more conservative era, but somehow the cycle had spun round again, after living through the rebellious spirit of the 1960s and the hippie generation that followed. He carried a sense of abandonment that had haunted him since his youth. The half of him now tasting the mystery of suffering, seeking a deeper, higher reality, and pondering the enigma of life over death. He wasn't alone in this; the philosophical, theological, and psychological musings of wiser men than him had wrestled with similar dilemmas through the ages.

Now here he was with the youth of today, more committed, perhaps unknowingly, to their rite of passage while still young. He, as the old man they had come to discuss the issues of coming to terms with their own upbringing, abandonments, and youthful wounds of the heart. This was something he, until then, had not come to terms with, and it was inspiring to feel a heartfelt camaraderie with them.

Perhaps it was the way they were there, a pilgrimage to a reported saint's tomb, the myth of it all, and the many myths that the Spanish villagers held dear, as they delved into the past to understand the myths they listened to in the present, trudging the weary way of the Camino. A rich insight for all in the rites of passage, sound guidance on those spheres of life when confronted with life's unanswered questions. Whilst myths in those rites of passage are not always easy to understand, it afforded the old man some glimpse into the mystery of it all, and a sense of growing into finding something constructive to cling to through it all, the frustrations of his former painful experiences. He could have easily become vain and bitter throughout his life journey. Still, somehow, those Camino journeys, particularly the first one, led him to deeper levels and potential enlightenment at the crossroads of his life.

The old man, now deep in thought, had come to understand the profound depths of life's mysteries. Paradoxically, he saw how the mythical tales in some way intertwined with his interpretations of reality. He had no reason to be disillusioned nor even bitter about what life had cast upon him, for life's bitter fruit he had tasted, and it gave him a greater understanding at a deeper level to cope with future crossroads that may come his way. At least, that's how he interprets it all, in the present day. He had come to believe and understand that the life mysteries he encountered led to the visions he was experiencing as progressive steps towards his connection with the guiding light of his Higher Power. There, he believed his strength was found, as his human soul was called upon to realise the meaning of life, if not the answer, embedded in what remained baffling.

The separation and loss the old man experienced throughout his life, while devastating to him, was a suffering that most humans must endure to a greater or lesser degree at some stage of their lives. Religious indoctrination, while explaining the sufferings of avatars like Buddha, Jesus, or Mohammad, had not eased his burden in that regard. It seems to him that much of his suffering was unfair or unmeritorious. Myth, unlike dogma, has never offered answers as to why we suffer, or how we may avoid it, or what God will give us in recompense.

In hindsight, he found some comfort in the transformative impact his suffering had on him, with glimpses of many myths hinting at a deep purpose embedded in his soul through those experiences that brought him the most pain. For in them, he discovered the way to heal by surrendering everything to the creator of all things.

Until he was transformed through the suffering of abandonment, family and material loss, and the depths of despair and loneliness in this world, spiritual healing could not occur. It arrived by peeling back the layers of myth via a lotus flower of creative ideas. His healing came not through his own needs or much effort, but through compassion for others, more than all the words he had written or the material gifts he had formally lavished upon himself as a reward for his effort. He no longer felt afraid of being alone, for there was some comfort in knowing that the power who knows all was his guiding spirit now. It was simply a matter of letting it all go and being open to the universe. He could not explain away the enigma of life's mysteries, for they still stood, and he knew there were no easy answers.

The gaining of wisdom had been lost on him for a long time. He had suffered much grief, and it took him a long time to navigate the complex stages of recovery. He had to confront his rage, despair, and the masks of his egocentric idealism; chasing after and capturing the women of the moment, the next golden emblem. He went through the depths of denial about his part in life turning pear-shaped for him, then guilt, shame, self-blame, blaming others, depression, and complete numbness of body and soul engulfed him before life turned from bitter to sweet again. He realised that he had done all the looking back he needed to do, and that he was not yet free from further darkness. This was a continuous process, rising and falling, like a boat on the sea of life, and he needed to be willing and prepared to accept it.

The old man often reflected on life before his fall and the aftermath of his tragic loss. He was mindful of the sad Greek tale of Orpheus and the loss of his beloved Eurydice, who died after being bitten by a snake [it possibly means the evil one].

Orpheus is a poet and musician whose playing of the kithara (a harp-like lyre) is so divine that the birds, the beasts, even the stones and the trees move to the rhythm of his songs. Shortly after his marriage to the nymph Eurydice, the newlyweds are cruelly parted when she dies after being bitten by a viper. Filled with grief, Orpheus cannot accept the loss of his beloved bride, and he decides to journey to the Underworld to bring her back. His musical talents charm Cerberus, the three-headed dog guarding the gates of hell, and enable him to reach the god of the Underworld, Hades, and his wife, Persephone. He also charms them with his song, and Hades tells Orpheus that he can take Eurydice back with him, with one condition: she must follow behind him as they leave the Underworld, and he must not look back at her. Overjoyed at being given this simple task, Orpheus thanks the gods and begins his ascent. But, unable to hear Eurydice's footsteps, he starts to worry that Hades has tricked him. As he nears the exit from the Underworld, he turns around to see Eurydice behind him, and she is lost forever. Heartbroken by this final separation and unable to return to the Underworld himself, Orpheus plays a mournful song on his lyre. His head remains intact and continues to sing as it floats away on the waters.

In his understanding of the myth, the old man realises how Orpheus strikes a deep chord within us all. It raised our hope that perhaps we can cheat death and avoid inevitable loss, and then it dashed that hope. Orpheus, like all men, has talents and a special gift, and we may feel that surely he, by perfecting his

art, or becoming rich and powerful, or being beautiful, or through enough good deeds and righteousness, could somehow be exempt from future grief or loss, or cheat death. The old man smiled at his thought that: 'Surely I, with thee I love, could be spared." He knew that this was impossible, for no one in life is spared from painful feelings of grief or sorrow; it cannot be avoided, and the experience of separation and loss does not discriminate between humans because of merit, even unto death.
The old man finally aligned his thoughts with the present day. He knew he must stop looking back because dwelling on the past only reopened old wounds of grief and loss. But can anyone honestly move forward without glancing behind? There might be a psychological renewal in this story. If we accept what has happened and learn from it, focusing on the present and the future, the losses we've left behind and the spirits of those from the past will be with us.

The myth talks of the certainty of endings, despite our attempts to cling to what has passed or to a creative spark that has inspired us. It offers no simple fix for dealing with loss, but it hints at the mysterious ways we can learn to let go. Still, if we delay and don't follow our inner spirit to let go honestly, these feelings might stay unless we actively seek closure. Otherwise, they could fade with us, which would be a shame because we wouldn't have grown through our experiences enough to reach the spiritual realm we are meant to pursue before our demise.

She stood there,
staring into space,
lost in her world,
along with pots and pans.

He came there,
climbing the stairs,

cried out to hold
took me in his arms.
Oh! Oh, we oh,
thinking of the past,
on some lonesome road,
best to let it go,

They were there,
hand in glove,
like two ships in the night,
never understood love.

He came there,
for a short time,
made her life worthwhile,
brother of mine.

It was there,
I was four,
We were so happy,
Then you just died.

Oh! Oh! We oh,
thinking of the past,
on some lonesome road,
best to let it go,

So many empty swings
in a child's playground.
So many empty swings
in a child's playground.

CHAPTER 6.

PEELING BACK THE LOTUS

Doctor Fred A. was a friend of Carl Jung. We shall continue to refer to him as Doctor Fred, as it would be unfair to compromise his anonymity. Now that he is deceased, I cannot ask for his permission to use his real name here. Suffice to say, he was my saviour during my times of great distress, when I was hospitalised with depression and extreme anxiety. In truth, it was more than that, for my suffering had been somewhat eased by my alcoholism. However, it eventually resurfaced, leading me to rehabilitation to dry out, regain my mental and physical health, and, although I didn't realise it at the time, address a spiritual ailment that was self-released through excessive drinking. It would take the slow work of God over the coming decade before I found my way back onto the path I still follow today.

The old doctor, like me, was an alcoholic who lay in the hospital bed next to mine. He wasn't suffering from the effects of drinking, but even though he was clean and sober, he was experiencing another bout of depression and was there to rest. [It would come to pass that I would have two more heavy episodes of depression and hospitalisation over the next decade before I would be free of this curse.]

After a lifetime as a leading psychoanalyst, Doctor Fred had the mental capacity to see what ailed me, and during my stay, he guided me with kind, wise, and spiritual words. He influenced the direction I would take in life more than any guidance I have received since. I recall Doctor Fred saying to me, towards the end of my hospitalisation: "You are a true die-hard alcoholic. How do I know this? Well, when you arrived here, I saw myself at your age, and I am a die-hard alcoholic too." He advised me to attend AA meetings and just let what was being shared there wash over me. I, having nothing better to do and feeling lost and a little lonely, started to attend AA meetings regularly. So the steps of AA are a daily practice in my life now, as they have been for the majority of the past eighteen years of sobriety.

While my recovery hasn't been a race to the finish line, it has been guided by golden threads of spiritual growth that have unravelled the coiled spring within me. I am learning each day to be honest with myself, open-minded, and willing to grow.

The old man, reminiscing about those days and his current state of mind, realised how much he was inspired by brave opportunities that led to his many adventures across Spain, Ireland, New Zealand, and on his Australian home front. He was now seeking the meaningful coincidences of his past that resonated with who he was and who he had become over the course of his lifetime. He was undoubtedly a loner, but no longer lonely, and an outsider who recognised similarities with others in his fellowship community.

He began to look back, visually examining his lifetime—who he was and had always been—long before he knew about the narrow, less travelled path compared to the one he had walked for decades before awakening to the spirit within. To catch a glimpse of life as it was, he started recalling the early days of his boyhood and what had changed for him, aiming to see what he had shaped himself into along the way, and what could be learnt for his betterment in the present and the future.

It was his birthday, as he remembered, a Tuesday, and whether it was a memory or a feeling, he knew he was alone and abandoned by his mother, who from the moment he was born had turned inward to the dark side of the moon. Another significant event that year was the start of the atomic age, with the bombing of Hiroshima and Nagasaki, which helped end World War II. He couldn't recall anything about that, as he was busy suckling from a surrogate mother's breast. It would be a maternal replacement act he would continue to gravitate towards for most of his life.

He recalled many fine moments from his childhood days. The sound of the baker's cart, winding its way up the hill with a big draught horse clip-clopping along, driven by Mr. French, delivering the baked bread of the day to the houses at the top where he lived with his parents and blood brother. Mr. French had been missing for a couple of years, as he had been incarcerated in Grafton Jail, several hundred miles to the north. The baker's cart wasn't in operation during those months; it was rumoured he had refused to pay his income tax, believing that his earnings were his own and that no taxation office or government, whether State or Federal, had any right to take his money. After all, what had they done for him to justify taking a part of his earnings? Let them earn their own money, was his attitude. Mr. French's stance and words had landed him in jail as a result. I wondered when I next saw him, for he seemed to be a more subdued man by then, whether he paid his taxes in future, or if he lived by bartering bread for other services. At any rate, he was still into the dough, so to speak.

The old man visualised the bell tower a stone's throw from his home, outside the Catholic church, and near the school he attended as a boy. It was a large single gong bell atop a telegraph pole. He recalled that it rang for the Angelus, a Catholic devotion centred around a prayer and the ringing of the bell, three times a day, to commemorate the Incarnation of Jesus Christ. The bell ringing serves as a call to worship and a reminder of the event when the Angel Gabriel announced to Mary that she would conceive the Son of God.

The nuns of a nearby convent rang the six o'clock in the morning bell, and on weekdays, the noon bell was rung by a schoolboy on a turnabout rotation. The old man remembered that he was always given the weekend duty of ringing the midday bell, living so close to the dang thing. The evening bell toll was again reserved for the nuns. He recalled being taught to ring the bell in the traditional pattern, with three rings, a pause for prayer, and a long peal of nine rings at the end. There was a long rope that rose to the bell, which hit the gong at the appropriate interval when pulled down by the bell-ringer.

The midday Angelus rang through that little village, into the valley below, and across the river that snaked its way through the town. He pictured a mechanic in a nearby garage stopping for a moment to listen to the tolling of the bell, a banker pausing in his counting, a barber, a butcher, the candlestick maker, a sawmill at the edge of town, a fisherman on the river, and the nearest farm. A workman stopped ploughing the field. All ceasing to pray the Angelus.

The tolling of that bell at six in the evening during his youth served as his reminder to be home for dinner. He could not recall when the Angelus bell stopped ringing but remembered his

"Angelus call" in the pubs when a six o'clock closing was the norm, and the barman called "Last drinks, gentlemen, please."

So many memories flood back then. Learning Latin for serving the Mass. Being taught, like his schoolmates, by a one-eyed, hungover priest of Irish persuasion who cracked a stock whip over their heads every time they got a Latin phrase wrong. The fun of riding and racing homemade billy carts down the steep hills, making slingshots to shoot at birds, and killing lizards with a pocket knife. Hiding behind a tree to jump out and chase after little girls for a kiss, not fully understanding the implications that would follow after puberty.

He was waking up in the shadow land again. Walking dusty through the streets of his childhood, seeing old faces ghostlike, now dead and gone. The old men on the bench in Midtown were chatting with passersby, knowing who was about their business—townsfolk shopping for household needs and a farmer or two in town for supplies and shackles. Each took time to catch up with the latest gossip, which the old men knew more about than the daily newspaper or the ABC radio. News that wouldn't make the print or the airwaves. Like, who the local barber was sleeping with this week, Mrs Kafoops, whilst her husband was at work, or old Bumpy on horseback, blind drunk as a skunk this morning, being guided like that by his blind horse. The old retired plumber sat outside his plumbing shop, surrounded by bits of leftover pipe and a few taps, odd ends. He stayed there selling these bits and pieces until he had collected enough shillings and pence to buy his daily couple of beers at the pub, which he walked to and from every day. The dentist then closed his surgery, on his way home for lunch break, still whistling happily as he had done on his way to the surgery earlier in the morning. What cold scenes he could see from those lives now dead and gone, which made him realise he had less time ahead than behind. It was no surprise that in his chats with friends over daily coffees at the local café, they often reminisced about their aches and pains, and how selfish the kids of today are compared to their youthful exuberance.

He was walking now in the shadow of the headstones in the lock graveyard, mindful of the fact that each headstone he passed bore the name, date of birth, and date of death of the bones that lay below the surface. "Ashes to ashes and dust to dust." He heard the priest's reminder during Good Friday Mass, as each of the indoctrinated had ashes placed on their foreheads with the timely reminder from the doomsayer priest: "Remember man that thou art dust and unto dust how shalt return."

No collection plate was passed round to support the priest, nor was there an offering for the church's upkeep that day. Easter Sunday came to mind when the priest climbed the pulpit stairs with a large register of collections, reading out the list of donations. "Mrs and Mrs Abbott, two pounds, Mr and Mrs Smith, ten shillings," and so on, making some parishioners swell with pride at their charity, while others fidgeted in shame for not being generous enough. Then the old man wondered why the Vatican couldn't look after the priest, God's poor, and the church themselves, instead of relying on the working class to pay for their sins with hard-earned cash. He remembered walking through the Vatican halls, viewing the Sistine Chapel, the gold and silver collections, and seeing money flowing like a waterfall from the rooftop into a collection pool below. He quickly dismissed the multitude of reasons why it was so. "ours is not to reason why ours is but to do or die."

Soon, the old man's thoughts wandered to the many friends he lost from his boyhood and, over the decades, those he had served with during his working life. He heard no more bells; all those ghostly images had faded away. Once again, he found himself on the beach, walking along the shoreline, reflecting on his life journey and why he always felt a sense of sadness and loneliness in the world. He never managed to figure it out in his boyhood. He was always busy with activity, but even among company, he felt alone.

He was unaware at the time that one day he would face the dragon at the base of his shadow self. To enter the dragon's mouth, and what would emerge would be a lotus flower of creative ideas. He looks back on all the living he had done and everything he needed to do before reaching that point, all the good he had done for his offspring, and all the failures and trials he had to endure before he would emerge as a creative self with awareness. For he was unaware that he would spend most of his life searching for the dragon, but the suffering he felt along the way, he tried to block out with drink, and driven by the need to lift his spirit to a goodly level, he sought the pleasures of fulfilling lustful desires, instead of turning to the God of his understanding within.

For a fleeting moment, he relived the sensation of Adam's rib, his image of a crucifixion engulfed in a maiden's breast. Naked bodies intertwined; the thrust of the sexual act, the waves of pleasure, the tide and splash upon the shore, then the thunderous wave exploding with volume as he drank the last of the lust. The womb of his desires drained the final of his vital fluids like the sand on the beach absorbing the remaining waters from the retreating wave.

He had the look of a young hero, once so much suffering had engulfed him, set off in search of the dragon. He had once been a figure of extreme intelligence—a giant, large, powerful, and commanding. Through the power of his own imagination, the dragon had transformed into a huge, loathsome, and sacred creature. The young man found the dragon in a cave within, and, going there with great fear and loneliness, turned once again to the pleasures of the flesh to escape that dark place inside. Most of the time, over the decades, the dragon slept, but it kept emerging from within him in the young man's dreams, enticing him to visualise a buried treasure underneath the dragon, buried deep below. He knew one day he would have to face the dragon, down in the depths of his cave, but it would only happen once he had surrendered his desires, given up the will, and let himself go there.

Ultimately, the young man, once old and no longer in need of material wealth, having endured the slings and arrows of outrageous fortune, no longer needed the presence of another female distraction or material possessions. He now recalled how he made his way to the inner cave on a wing and a prayer, for he wanted nothing from what the world could offer but what truly lay hidden within himself and the dragon's mouth buried deep inside the dragon cave. He carried a spiritual sword of discernment, a presence of the spirit's power like a flaming sword, reminiscent of the sword of St. James the Apostle, who symbolically led the Christians into battle in 800 AD. He remembered how he had come to free fall into the dragon's mouth, which had turned into a lotus flower of creative ideas that sustained him with his writings of books and songs up to his present old age. He now knew that his writings and songs were merely residual parachutes of what his real desire now was. He had slain the mythical dragon within, but his holy grail still awaited him from the depths of the dragon's cave, and he needed three things for his adventure—without fear or favour, without any mythical shadow self, or the need for a residual parachute like he once needed. He was freer now, able to let bygones be bygones.

He realised the dragon had been a creature born from his own human greed and lingering inertia. He discovered that the wealth beneath the dragon was simply accepting his spiritual essence, which was his true worth. He no longer needed to use it for his pleasure or pursuits, but in giving of himself to others. Due to his good intent, he gained much spiritual power and a freedom he had never known before.

The old man no longer valued material wealth as he once thought he needed. Because the challenges of his life had taught him deep self-awareness, he faced the reality of human cruelty. He had reclaimed and renewed his inheritance in a spiritual, rather than material, way. He had found integrity. Now, he understood what mattered most to him: not superficial pleasures, luxury, or worldly gold. He only owed himself the protection of an unseen spirit, which came from surrendering to a higher power—something he didn't bother to define but trusted and believed in. He didn't seek to explain its significance to others; for him, it was enough to live by its guidance, content to let others find their own path, whether towards the divine or not.

I know my heart beats to a drummer
That's not quite the same as the rest
It's where I long to be
attuned with the sound in my chest.

Listen to the rhythm of the heartbeat
the sound of a different drum
nit the beat of a heart for another
nor the weary heart wounded by love.

It won't be found in worldly values
where money's the ultimate quest
not the best of a heart in battle
where they pin a medal on your breast.

It may be found in nature
where man is alone with the plan
climbing a rugged mountain range
tilling and planting the land.

Sailing the blue of the ocean
viewing the flight of a bird
hearing the sound of cicadas
deep in a forested wood.

Catching a fish for survival
cooking it on one's fire
sleeping out in the open
watching a star-filled sky.

Seeing the sunrise at dawn
plainly being in tune
living the now when it's crowded
being quite still in a room.

CHAPTER 7.

FAIR MAIDENS, FOWL DEEDS.

It was, in fact, a symbol of worldly wisdom, for with it all men could tell when to be still, when to observe, and when to voice opinions to others. To the old man, it represented the ability to know and keep the secret, without which those who saw themselves as wise adults were just children who blurted out everything they felt to anyone willing to listen. To the old man, that was artificiality; it was the way he used to be, but it was no longer. He had learnt, though, the bittersweet lessons that he must be as gentle as a lamb in all his material dealings, but as vigilant as a female serpent when it came to dealing with the fairer sex.

So it was that the old man remembered the myth of his youth, where he had been in his imagination a brave knight of the realm, begging the king to send him on a quest of his choosing to prove his worth. The king's muse within him was both enemy and friend, an enemy whom he helped capture one of his fair maidens, and a motivator who turned his adventurer into a knight of the castle where the maiden was held captive. Along the way, he encountered two of the king's enemy knights, his shadow self of devastation and despair, whom he quickly defeated in an imagined sword fight to the death, and a foe of spiritual detention whom, though many trials, he ultimately defeated. He had entered the castle but found no maiden, only a fire-breathing dragon. He was inspired by a voice from the spirit world to kiss the dragon on the lips, whereupon the dragon turned back into the maiden, who had been bewitched by the king's enemy, a powerful witch indeed.

On his adventurous journey, chasing the maiden and meeting many more, he grew up, proving to be a brave knight, marrying the maiden and fathering many children. And when she had done with him, she left him for another, leaving him a sad but wiser knight as a consequence.

He had been enticed to a new maiden's crystal garden, set in a garden of delicate spices and flowers which bloomed in all seasons. The maiden who lived there had loved him from afar but did not know him, and equally, he did not know her.

He arrived at her castle at night, where he was to fight the castellan for what could be called a night's lodgings. Or if he managed to meet and sleep with the maiden, then it would truly be a knight's proper lodgings. He found her while the castellan, hired to protect her virginity, slept soundly at the entrance gate. He had been unaware that she had arranged with the king to send him on the adventure to find her. However, while he did enjoy the pleasures of the night with her, he found himself the next day having to fight knight after knight who came to defend her honour. He, at the end of the day, had won through to take his fair maiden and leave with her. He proved his valour and fell asleep in her arms, only to soon discover to his dismay that he could no longer hold her love, and before long, as it was morning, he woke alone in the woods, armour-clad and with a horse by his side. He had dreamed that he returned victorious to marry her, take over the kingdom, and live happily ever after, but it was all just a dream.

The old man realised that the dream was his own search for identity, which still haunted him despite the progress he had made. He understood that he knew himself better now, just as most young men— including the one in his dream— had not yet discovered who they truly were to become. The lesson of leaving the safety of familiar shores to sail and conquer unknown destinations was an inward journey of self-discovery, away from the comfort of past experiences. In his dream, filled with many myths—a fight with a dragon—whether it involved the fear of overcoming the fire from the dragon's mouth or kissing it, was a call to conquer evil. The dragon symbolised his greed and a former life of chaos and destruction; the demons on his path represented the need to destroy everything, including the lust for the fair maiden, before he could prove himself a worthy knight, a brave soldier of spiritual strength.

The dreamer's task was not to kill the dragon but to tame the creature, break its spell over him, and restore it to its true purpose. He learnt from the dream that compassion and understanding would achieve far more than rage or suppression in the fight against inner chaos.

The old man recognised that his duty was not to win over people's hearts or to be stubborn and unrepentant, for he had read and been guided by the verses of the Bible that it would ultimately only provoke God's wrath. "God will repay each person according to what they have done, for those who persist in doing good seek glory, honour and immortality. He will give eternal life. But for those who are self-seeking, reject the truth, and follow evil, there will be wrath and anger." [Romans 2: 6-8] The world he knew was full of deception, and he realised how tempting it was to be among those he now saw as the living dead—those who had died inside because they had succumbed to inner despair and darkness. This, he saw, was hell on earth, where there was no love, compassion, or joy in their hearts, which is why they are rotting in the eyes of God.

The old man had pushed himself so hard throughout his life to fit into society's ways for power, material wealth, and applause, only to find it all amounted to nothing. His real burden wasn't his writings, songs, and utterances for worldly recognition—things he once thought defined him-but rather to overcome evil, which not only existed in the world but also within his own flawed character. He still carried impulsive and regressive urges, and facing these took courage and understanding. Overlooking his own shortcomings, he needed to serve others out of the generosity of his heart, rather than giving in to the weaknesses of his nature for lustful pleasures and vain glory.

He once believed he would reach his full potential through marriage to a nymph of his own making, have children, and settle into a way of life that fulfilled what he thought God had intended for him. It was not to be, for she was merely a creature of fantasy who ultimately went her own way, as did his offspring. He sometimes thought that the bloom of his life would blossom into a vibrant garden of colour and awe-inspiring brilliance. Still, instead, it had ultimately proved to be the lingering fragrance of peeling back a lotus flower of creative ideas that he was meant to pursue. But even this was coming to an end, too. The ideal that inspired him to reach his full creative potential, for good, for truth and beauty, by its very nature could never be entirely achieved. And he realises that if he dwells too long in the realm of his imagination, he may ignore the outer world, which requires his efforts and attention. He knew, as time passed in the afternoon of his life, that he needed both ideals and a sense of reality, for like all men, he must come to terms with living life here and now and must find his own identity within the framework of being human.

He was reminded, on the anniversary of his son's death, of life's brevity and how youthful exuberance often fell victim to death's traps, for they lacked the wisdom of age. And then the death of so many of his mates, who, by fate, unexpected illness, or what seems unfair, had died before fulfilling their desires.

He mourned not only because he missed them but also because he was reminded of his mortality and that he, too, would one day die. He had once been a man of clear courage, but he also lost his way, yet fought back and was admired for his bravery. He had reached an age where it mattered little to him anymore, even though it once did. He was seen as a model for the ideal adventurer, a pilgrim well-versed in the routes, myths, and legends of the Camino de Santiago, about which he had written many fine tales. The old man had concluded that he could no longer sit around pondering the ultimate fate of humanity, any more than he could his own mortality. He knew of Noah's long life, which spanned the great flood and was marked by his being chosen by God to warn humankind to repent and be saved. The story mirrored the ancient Babylonian tale of Utnapishyim, who also survived the flood and found immortality.

The old man had walked many pilgrimages in his lifetime, partly in search of the long life he had now experienced, and partly on a spiritual quest to find his grail—to live by the guidance and uncover the remaining secrets of life and death. He had, at the start of his wanderings, come to the foot of the Pyrenees Mountains guided by an inner spirit, and there was a reminder of the dangers of walking the Camino Way in midsummer, for all sorts of dangers lay on the trail, from deadly snakes to scorpions. A misguided fool on the trail tried to dissuade him from stepping out on the old trail, warning that it was not only dangerous because of serpents, mythical dragons, witches, and warlocks he described in great detail, but also because the trail ahead on the mountain had been partly blocked by a landslide. The old pilgrim was not deterred, for he had faced many more real dangers, sufferings, and misfortunes in his time, and he believed this one had more to do with his future path than any of his past tramping. He was, after all, an old man, having lived his time, and if it was the wish of a power greater than himself that he should die, then he considered it no less than a great honour that he might die on the pathway where St. James himself had reportedly ventured to preach in support of his risen Christ that "Faith without works is dead,"

He had warned the man of a dangerous omen that he was on a quest to discover the life that God had planned for him now. The misguided fool, with some sense of admiration, let this hero pass. So it was that the old man climbed the mountain high and into the valley below, arriving at a place of rest by nightfall—a quiet chapel.

He slept well and left early in the morning to find some food at a nearby inn to fuel his body for the day ahead. There, the women of the inn tried to dissuade him from his journey. "Where do you want to go, old man?" she asked. He soon realised that she was one of those who were afraid to set out for herself, viewing life as a glass half empty, whereas he saw it as a glass half full. She spoke with authority like a witch would, "You shall not find what you're seeking." Then, with a cackle and a cock-eyed smile, "When the Gods created man, Death was his allotment, not immortality." He did not respond to her words, for she let down the top of her blouse to expose a well-formed breast. It was not that she wasn't pretty; she was. It was the fact that he had so often fallen for female anatomy in the past, in preference to his mission, for she no longer enticed him as she was, for he was on a quest of his own making. He had resolved to keep the secret of his quest to himself. He had his fill of food and paid the women handsomely.

He walked through the heat of the day until he reached a river, where he bathed in the cool, flowing stream. There, he heard music drifting from a nearby village, so he headed there, revelling in the dance, singing, and festivities with others of his kind- free spirits on their journey.

He returned to the path beside the river, where he met a boatman whom the old man instructed to ferry him across the waters of death to a nearby island. It was a place of guidance where he found a tree of life, knowledge, and love, but he knew its essences and lessons were in its leaves, if he would only chew on them. He also sensed that they might not only be filled with all he desired, but in fact, a serpent lay at the base of the tree. He surmised that death might follow, so he declined to eat the leaves of the tree of life, perhaps believing that in making himself young again, he might die of snake poison as a consequence. He crossed back over the sea of death once more to the place he had come from, knowing that despite his weakness, physical ailment, and sense of loss for all he once cherished, he had to move on to complete the quest he had set himself. He had long ago concluded that even though he might be courageous and had once been a hero, he still had to learn to live with joy in the present moment and accept an inevitable end at his appointed time.

He had faced many successes and just as many losses, realising that life at its best was still unfair. He had lost friends and borne the heaviness of cruel fate, especially losing his beloved son by his own hand. His only explanation for his fate was that it was the will of the gods. He often thought about his parents, and in particular, his most beloved grandfather, but he also thought about old school friends and work colleagues who had passed away.

It was perhaps death that constantly reminded him of humankind's lot; the hardships many face, a direct confrontation with illness, and the tough circumstances that upset his own life, scattering his plans and dreams to the four winds of change.

He had refused the part in his youth to face the inevitable, like all young men, to accept his fate. He had been a hero, conquered monsters, and made his mark in the world. The gift of the first half of his life had filled him with confidence and a sense of specialness, until it all started to go pear-shaped. That was until he lost everything: family, material wealth, home, and friends. He had picked up the pieces and rebuilt relationships, gained new friends, and found the freedom to do as he pleased with his life. He felt that if he was lucky, he might return to that part of his life he had so easily squandered, with good times coming his way. As he grew older, he surmised that the path he now walked might be more subtle, a test of his resilience and ability to conquer anything. He was, however, mindful that such an attitude on his quest might clash with the reality of what is reserved for the gods alone.

Yes, he needed to challenge life, just as he did when he was young, but now with the wisdom gained from facing life as an old man. He had already achieved many of his goals, and he had to avoid clinging to childish behaviour; instead, he challenged life no matter what it presented him. He must resign himself to his fate while living in the spirit of his destiny, not in the way the world tries to bind him. He was now mindful that there were some boundaries he could not cross, some fates that his belief in were his inner guidance. He had to stop thinking like all he did was of worldly consequence and focus on what his inner spirit, linked to his Maker, was guiding him towards.

He had reached a point where he could face worldly challenges for the benefit of others without considering his own advantages. If any act he might perform from now on placed his efforts in the realm of heroism, he knew he could channel this within the limits of his talents and his unique gift of personality. It was now for him to explore life's mysteries, which he had been learning about through his writings. While he remained somewhat aloof from his emotional response to this way of life, he was aware of the sense of compassion that had been generated. Detachment from worldly desire and understanding spiritual realities was now his lot. It was true that his conscious goals were fading as his youthful nature faded too—fading light of egocentric behaviour was replaced with the beckoning lily of magic from the spiritual, not the passion of his former years, but a quiet, slow, step-by-step impetus towards what fate had in store for him now.

There's a boatman who rows the river,
across the Ganges deep and wide,
carrying passengers for rupees,
to reach the other side.

The pay is very meagre,
He rows by day and night,
and the waters can be dangerous,
It depends upon the tide.

He rows to feed his family,
and he rows to keep his pride,
carrying passengers for rupees,
And he'll do that till he dies!

Children working on the river,
across the Ganges deep and wide,
clearing garbage from the riverbank,
just to stay alive.

Now the boatman's coming for me,
to take me for a ride,
to a land of milk and honey,
In a kingdom on the other side.

He's coming for the living,
on the last day that I survive,
So I'm waiting by the river,
waiting for a change of tide,

Oh! Boatman, stay away today
I'd rather stay alive,
pass me over for another day,
Take another upon the tide.

The river runs quickly,
boatmen row with pride,
ferrying passengers by the hundreds,
to get to the other side.

Now I dream of a flowing river,
milk and honey deep and wide,
If a boatman comes to take me,
in a paradise of my desire.

Oh! waiting at the river's edge,
old Buddha takes my hand,
and he leads me beside still waters,
into the promised land.

Jesus standing next to him,
with a rosary by his side,
praying with stigmata wrists,
Whilst the throng strikes up the band.

Mother Mary is close by,
with a snake under her foot,
smiles gently at this mortal soul,
Checks me in the book of life!

So I'm led beside still waters,
beyond a babbling brook,
to meet the Master of the universe,
On a hilltop, we overlook.

In the teeming, flowing millions,
they are all there like sheep,
There are no tears or hunger,
just playful without a bleep.

The shepherd leads the flock now,
contented with his lot,
in a land of joy and wonder,
with lush grass and no upkeep.

 My next of kin surrounds me,
with friends and lovers too,
In a land of milk and honey,
and children at my feet.

Oh! I awake from dreaming,
by the river Ganges roar,
see the starving teeming millions,
wanting to know their score.

In the book of life, many meanings,
These we will get to know,
The day the boatman comes for men,
beyond the overflow.

Now the boatman's coming for me,
to take me for a ride,
to a land of milk and honey,
in a kingdom on the other side.

Oh! Boatman, stay away today
I'd rather stay alive,
pass me over for another day,
Take another on the tide.

The river Ganges is long and deep,
The rivers deep and wide,
There's teeming, starving millions,
wanting to get to the other side.

CHAPTER 8.

LOVE

As a traveller on the path of emotional sensation and the awareness of love's loss, won and lost forevermore, I can now endorse the statement with some authority: it is love that truly makes the world go round. The reality of love is not a myth, for it is hard-fought and involves realigning oneself with another without fear or favour. Throughout life, we find that many myths surround the true essence of love. The myths of marriage and separation, love and rivalry, sexual fidelity and infidelity, and the ultimate understanding of the transcendent powers of compassion that underpin the importance of love are ever present throughout history. No variation exists in the theme of relationships that cannot be found in myth. This is because human relationships are complex, just as the morality that myths portray is multifaceted.

It remains a mystery why people are attracted to or repelled by each other, and why we seek simple answers to questions that are so complex and require a deep understanding even to formulate. A reasonable answer to such an enquiry.

In his lifetime, the old man had experienced love, the pain of losing a loved one, and the misguided lure of lust instead of love that left him not only broken and deep in despair but also challenged his belief in the very existence of love. His life has been a myth in itself, as is the adopted belief in a power greater than himself. So, it is with myth here that he uses it more as a catalyst to embrace the essence of love—the moral lessons that these 'mythical tales' offer about love; to provide some solace in one's unhappiness, serve as a guiding light through the dilemma, and offer a sorely needed insight into what we need to do in our personal lives to recapture the lessons of love, or indeed find it without misgiving for the first time.

Let's suppose there was once a young man who, although he felt love in his heart, couldn't express it to anyone except through his poetry—a shadow nymph of his imaginings. She was the object of his desire, the one he was searching for, a pure soul, a prototype of his idea. It wasn't until his later youth that he experienced it physically, with infrequent kissing and encounters with young women he met. They all came to know him for a while. While each one in turn embraced the youth affectionately, they had no idea he wanted a proper relationship or the idea of his desire to deflower their virginity, which he didn't fully understand himself at the time.

So here was a sexual passion of unmatched imagination, depicted as a myth within this youth. A force mightier than any of his real experiences, capable of pushing any human or god into actions against their will or better judgment. Such indifference to passion and lustful urges could only lead to tragedy. It was the image of the goddess that would trouble any man when he gazed upon such a woman as in his dreams.

So it followed for this youth, who soon became wayward in passion, madness, and destruction, due to his uncontrolled desire for a beautiful nymph whose need for sexual satisfaction was even greater than his own. It led him down a path of conflicting moral forces that ultimately drained his physical strength, eroded his courage to face reality, and damaged his natural soul, leaving him in turmoil. It was not a relationship of godly-inspired love; it was not safe. Myth taught him the extent to which passion overwhelmed consciousness, leaving only a real source of hurt, rejection, and even catastrophe.

Although the young man looked wonderful on the surface, his shadow self had grown dark, depressive, and blind to the beauty of nature. He turned to other pleasures like drugs and alcohol to calm the savage beast inside. A wake-up call would eventually come, but not before he was dragged through hell for quite some time. As a result, he became a very self-absorbed young man.

He took to walking alone in the woods, just like he did as a kid. There, he ran into another woman of mythical proportions. She seemed to love him but never came too close, afraid she might be the one to lift him out of his blues. Eventually, he stopped by a lake to quench his thirst, and that's when the nymph revealed herself. She shed her clothes and urged him to do the same. The young man was now struck by the beauty of the purest of creatures and said how her beauty moved him. In response, the nymph suggested the young man undress like her and take a swim in the lake. So it was that the young man, for the moment forgetting his melancholy, disrobed and jumped into the water, eager to do whatever this vision of hers required. She also drew closer and swam up to him, wrapping her body around him and almost overpowering him with her passionate kiss.

When the lustful passion of the two youths had faded, they dressed and sat by the lake. It was then that he realised he had been caught in the allure of her beauty, which he saw for the first time in the still surface of the lake. Then, gazing upon his own reflection rather than that of the nymph he had just deflowered, he came to see that he was beautiful too. She was upset that he had taken her so easily and seemed less interested in her now that the lustful act was over. It was an essential mythic lesson for the young man: love can only be found in giving, not in taking. For each of them, in their own way, there was a focus on their desires from the other, and love could only happen when mutual. Love existed, as their pattern was now set, that one could never truly trust that love would come in the future if past lustful acts were the basis for any future sexual encounters.

He had not yet learnt the lesson of revealing his heart to himself because he was too self-absorbed to have the maturity at the time to do so. He went through life for an extended period repeating the fulfilment of lustful desires before he became aware of being honest with himself. It took marriage, its breakdown, and separation before he developed healthy self-esteem. He had learnt to become someone who was special and loved by someone who cared, not in an idolised fantasy of perfection. The young man took until his later years to realise that lustful mythical loves were of others' unreality, and love, whether of oneself or another, is two opposites of the same coin, so to speak.

The now wise old man, reflecting on the myth and reality of the young man's sexual exploits, saw in them evidence of lessons learnt the hard way, which echoed his own upbringing, not only revealing his immaturity as a youth but also highlighting how his own parenthood and that of those who brought him into the world were equally lacking in love.

The old man was recalling the biblical story of Samson — how he gained great strength through his hair, his involvement with an unsuitable wife, his sexual encounters with Delilah as his mistress, and how he had mistakenly revealed his secrets, which were given to him by God, to a woman — something that was against his benefit and that of his people. He had erred by firstly choosing an unsuitable wife, and secondly as King and judge by aggravating the enmity between the Israelites and the Philistines, then thirdly through his passion for Delilah, another of his many unsuccessful lovers, and then even more importantly, revealing the God-given secret to his mistress of how he gained his strength through the length of his hair, which was symbolic of an expression of his confidence in God and belief. Samson paid for his indiscretion, for he was an angry man. He abused the 'Spirit of the Lord,' which moved him to excess in arguments, making him violent and self-willed. Like many Greek heroes, Samson lacks self-restraint and therefore does not seek to control what drives him from within. When he wants something, he must have it, and that includes taking a wife from his enemies. Love is not at issue here, but passion fueled by physical attraction, driven by his instinctive need for gratification. When he tires of his wife, he dismisses her. When her father, reasonably, refuses to give her back, he causes chaos in the Philistines' wheat fields, and tragedy follows. Samson is not a friendly character. He is violent, stubborn, and unfeeling. He is the architect of his own downfall.

For Sampson, temptation is destined to succeed, as he has no capacity for reflection. He is not suspicious of Delilah's persistence because his emotions and instincts drive him. In the end, he reveals all to her, and this costs him his strength.

Hair—short, long, dark, or pale—features prominently in many of the world's myths and carries symbolic weight. Historically, its significance is clear; for example, the Merovingian kings of France did not cut their hair because they believed it signified their divine right to rule. Freud associated hair with feelings of impotence. However, aside from Freud's views, it's worth noting that Sampson's strength comes from the hair on his head, symbolising the mind. Hair can represent one's thoughts; it acts as a symbol of personal reflection, shaping and guiding one's will and worldview. Our strength, at its core, lies in our ability to think, perceive the world, and process it through our consciousness. Only then can we control our destructive impulses and avoid falling into blind emotion. By giving in to physical passion, Sampson relinquishes his independent sense of self. His hair is symbolically lost long before it is physically cut because he neglects the power of reflection to nourish his passions. His downfall lies in the way he freely abandons all capacity for reflection.

Therefore, Sampson's blindness is a myth used to link understanding with avoiding the outside world. It is only when he is struck in prison that Sampson begins to look inward, and what does he find? His hair grows back; he gains the ability for thought and reflection; he prays to the God he had forgotten for forgiveness; and his strength returns.

The understanding of this old man in the Sampson myth is that, in our failings, we recognise who we truly are and whom we serve at the end of the day. We, as humans, need to balance blind power with insight, reflection, and our core values that drive us. Through our mistakes, messes, and hurts we inflict and receive, and through pursuing our passions with reflection, we hurt ourselves and others. Through humility, new awareness is forced upon us to turn inward, to regain strength and recover our individuality. Sampson's detachment is symbolic as a humble recognition that we must undergo a sort of death in our transition to new life. We must let go of our arrogance and self-will, and recognise life's limitations. The story of Sampson reveals the inner transformative effects of passion, which lead us from suffering to inner self-revelation and a new understanding of ourselves and life.

The old man had come to realise that, as a young bloke, he could rationalise and intellectualise most things, especially in the pursuit of power, job titles, material success, and sexual gratification. However, when it came to his passions, it was never from the heart; it was all in his head, and there was no antidote for love within him. Although he started to reflect, he couldn't silence his heart or body with reason alone. In fact, trying to use reason as a defence against passion only made him more vulnerable and blinded him to his then-relationships.

So it came to pass that the old man remembered the legendary Merlin in the days of King Arthur and his Knights. Merlin was King Arthur's mentor, adviser, and mate, using his power to tap into the Universe's magical energies. Not only was he skilled in herbal medicine, but he was also a visionary who could see into the future. He could change shape and transport himself telepathically, appearing in non-places and then in different spots and forms. He didn't indulge in love or lustful exploits, choosing instead to focus his energies on his magical work for King Arthur and the court of Camelot.

While Merlin was highly skilled, he did not fully know himself. Yet, this wise and self-assured enchanter met his match in the honey trap of love and desire. He fell for a beautiful maiden named Nyneve and, despite being an old bloke by then, he was head over heels in love with her. To impress her, he took the form of a dashing young lad and boasted of his magic prowess. He conjured fabulous illusions out of thin air, aiming to win her admiration. Knights, ladies of the court, minstrels, and flowers appeared as he willed them. The proud women watched silently.

Merlin was so absorbed in his imagination and busy trying to impress that he didn't notice the young Nyneve wasn't returning his feelings. Still, she promised to become his lover if he shared her magical secrets. Eagerly, he agreed, trusting in her loyalty both as a devoted follower and as his lover. Nyneve then coaxed more knowledge from him, learning all his spells and magical recipes, but she kept herself at arm's length, frustrating his hopes. Merlin, with his wisdom, gradually realised what was going on and knew he was being tricked and deceived. But he couldn't help himself.

Seeing clearly what the future held, he went to King Arthur to warn him that the end was near for his trusted adviser and enchanter. The king was baffled as to why Merlin, with all his wisdom, was trapped by this woman and could do nothing for himself. Merlin responded: "It is true, I know many things. Yet in the battle between knowledge and passion, knowledge never wins."

Merlin was like a lovestruck kid, burning with passion and desire; he followed Nyneve everywhere. Yet the woman never gave in to his wishes, always promising and tempting him but never granting what he wanted, which only made him more secretive. Eventually, he made the mistake of teaching her the secret cells that can never be broken. To please her, he carved a magical chamber into the grand Cornish cliffs high above the sea and filled it with incredible wonders. He intended it to be a beautiful place where they might finally come together. When they approached the chamber, it was adorned with gold and lit by hundreds of scented candles. Merlin went inside, while Nyneve lingered outside. Then she spoke the words of a terrible spell that could not be broken, a spell she had learnt for him.

The door to the chamber closed, and Merlin was trapped inside forever. As Nyneve moved away down the passage, she could hear his voice faintly through the rock, begging to be released. But she paid no mind and kept walking. It's said that Merlin still stays there in his gold-hung chamber, just as he knew he would.

Merlin, like many others, used his sharp intellect and knowledge to control life instead of truly experiencing it and allowing himself to be changed by it. When we desperately seek something, we tend to lose control and become vulnerable to whatever life throws at us. For those of us wounded in childhood, we learn early on to mistrust love; both the age we recognise it and the wrong age can serve as shields to avoid hurt. However, such defence leaves us childlike and naive deep down until we confront the truth of our feelings and pass through experiences of frustration and separation, which can ultimately guide us to maturity. Otherwise, we might end up like Merlin—exposed to exploitation.

In daily life, we may doubt ourselves and try to impress others with our strength, wealth, talent, or knowledge, not realising that, by betraying our true selves, we could be opening a door to regret and pain. When we present ourselves as something we're not, we deceive—either intentionally or unconsciously—and in doing so, we also invite deception.

The story of Merlin warns us about the risks of passion when someone lacks genuine self-belief and avoids true equality, which real love needs. In the story of Samson, the biblical hero is only in touch with his physical urges and doesn't have the ability for deep reflection. Meanwhile, Merlin is fearful of bodily desires and trusts only his mind. A balance between the two

is vital for maintaining mental health and fostering a meaningful relationship.

Love.

Is it the sound I'm hearing in the trees?
Do I see you in the falling leaves,
maybe it's the sweetness of the breeze,
 the feel of sand between my toes.

We did our mating in some distant past,
Life was always splendid in the grass,
Now feelings are faded memories,
And nothing ever lasts for long.

Is it the woman cradled in my arms,
the warmth of her constant charms,
maybe it's the child upon my lap,
that sense of innocence.

Oh! Love,
Come back into my room,
and take away these blues.

Did I catch you out of the corner of my eye?
The shadow of the bird flying by,
the warmth of the sun upon my face,
maybe now in a fading cloud.

Did I see you somewhere on the road?
Was it a gentle hand upon my back,
maybe it's the burden of the load,
When I look back.

Oh! Love
Come back into my room,
and take away these blues.

CHAPTER 9.

THE LAST HURRAH

Hence, the old man started thinking about another Camino de Santiago. One might wonder why an eighty-year-old would want to undertake another tough pilgrimage to a distant land. He had been reconsidering that for a while, thinking about his current health, the wear and tear on his body, and whether it made sense to do it again in his later years. The previous three Camino journeys had been tough with health and emotional hurdles. Still, they all brought new life experiences, and he felt he needed to do a SWOT analysis (Strengths, Weaknesses, Opportunities, and Threats) to judge whether his decision was wise.

In Biblical history, Jesus apparently showed his disciples that he must go to Jerusalem on Mount Zion to the temple to fulfil his prophecy of suffering and spiritual resurrection. In contrast, the Camino de Santiago ends at the renowned site of the same name, but the cathedral itself isn't on a "high hill"; instead, the city, set amid the lush landscape of Galicia, can be reached after crossing hills and valleys, and the cathedral rises to dominate the city skyline as pilgrims arrive. It also has a connection with Jesus through his Apostle James, who is believed to have travelled along the Way preaching the message of the Risen Christ, exemplified by the phrase "Faith without works is dead." For over a thousand years, pilgrims have walked this path to spiritually shed their burdens and celebrate at a Pilgrims' Mass at the journey's end, at the tomb of St. James, beneath the altar in the Cathedral.

So here was the old man, reminiscing about his three Camino pilgrimages over the past decade. One was of personal hardship in letting go of life's burdens, another of experiencing regrets over lust rather than love and the lessons learnt from those times, and the final long, winding journey of nearly 1200 kilometres on his third trip. This included walking from Santiago to Cape Finisterre, then across the Sea to Ireland to climb the Wicklow Mountains, explore the Aran Islands, follow the Barrow Way, and return to scale mountain ranges in New Zealand.

He had done it all, documented his journeys in novels and songs, and learnt to let go of much of what he once believed was important. Despite his creative efforts, his dissatisfaction with life made him consider returning to the Camino once more. It was no longer about releasing past pain and suffering, or ideas for some creative project; it was no longer about bedding a foreign beauty, nor about the satisfaction of completing another pilgrimage. Although he had left a legacy of many creative works, it was no longer about feeling fulfilled in achieving things, because all these fade away in the mist of time and ultimately mean little in the grand scheme. He, too, would eventually be dust and perhaps remembered on the anniversary of his death by family or friends, but to what purpose for those left to reflect on his life? A headstone in a grave, like any other man in the spirit world beyond life.

The old man was now reflecting on how his final Camino would focus more on surrendering to what he was guided to do each day, highlighting the meditative aspects of walking The Way. He was thinking about how he had spent the following eight years after his last Camino writing short stories and recording even more songs. Eventually, he reached a point where he didn't need to do anything besides get through the day, catch up with mates over a coffee, and chat about life, the self-imposed limitations, and physical constraints that naturally come with ageing.

So here he was at eighty, contemplating another Camino de Santiago. He naturally hesitated at the idea of walking such a distance at his age, but something within sparked his spirit, and he started to think about it more deeply. He considered the thought that he had no need to prove himself to anyone, of the pride of achievement, or passionate desires, for now he was his own man, free from any restraints. He knew that he could be in the world but not of the world. He had made all the amends he considered necessary for others. It was hard to let go of his defective nature, and while he still knew there was more to peel back and release, he concluded that it would all happen in God's time, not his own. He saw it now that his pilgrimage would be to learn the way of the spirit in meditative walking, compassion for his fellow pilgrims, and the hope that he would fulfil the task and hopefully not die along the Way as he had recalled the experiences of many monuments of fallen heroes of the Way who had died there.

This ageing man was now contemplating the "price of freedom" to walk The Way again as he pleased. Such a phrase emphasises that maintaining freedom demands effort, vigilance, and sometimes sacrifice. It appears across many contexts, including historical events, fictional tales, and debates about societal values. He remembered that wars, revolutions, and other conflicts are often fought to gain or safeguard freedom from oppression or tyranny. He also recalled that many people have historically faced hardship, risked their lives, or endured great suffering to fight for or defend freedom. The cost of defending freedom and advancing liberty can be substantial. Protecting freedoms like speech, religion, assembly, and fundamental rights is essential for a truly free society. Active participation in politics and holding leaders accountable are also crucial. This old man saw freedom as having both external value and spiritual significance. While he recognised freedom's worldly importance, history has demonstrated that human nature complicates its true realisation. For him now, it was more about living life freely and letting God be his guiding force. And would his hopes of freedom bring him happiness in walking the Camino again? Well, he had pondered that too.

In his search for his place in life, he had changed jobs, got married, and, driven by forces he couldn't control, taken geographical cures and ran himself into debt financially, emotionally, and spiritually. He had learnt to grow up and realised that weight, people, places, or things could make him happy and set his heart free. He had realised, though, after following the steps of Alcoholics Anonymous and having given up alcohol, that when problems overwhelmed him, the AA steps helped him grow through his pain and difficulties. As the AA co-founder Bill Wilson once said: "When pain comes, we are expected to learn from it willingly, and help others to learn also. What happens comes, we accept as a gift, and thank God for it."

Once, material values ruled his life, especially when he drank excessively. He thought that possessions would bring him happiness. Over time, he found a new way of living, centred around walking the Camino for the first time, as it was then that his mindset shifted from worldly logic to one of curiosity and creativity in harmony. He started to trust the freedom that comes with opening up to God spiritually. The gifts of the Spirit gradually replaced material pursuits as a result. This didn't happen quickly, as he had many worldly habits to let go of. He remembered the words of a wise counsellor who, when he had lost everything—wife, family, friends, and business—and the will to go on: "Congratulations, you are now on your spiritual path. God is leading you, trust in his slow work." It proved true, and now, some decades later, after many adventures in his search for answers, in writing countless words in books and songs, it all led to one realisation: that none of it was truly important, apart from acceptance and humility in letting go of the world, and being disciplined to step forward, open to whatever God had planned for him and his role in the wider world.

This retiree from worldly pursuits had considered his bucket list of remaining dreams, goals, and experiences he wanted to achieve before he passed away. He had undertaken many of the thrilling adventures that involved taking risks and saw no need to push his luck further at his age; activities like learning to play a new instrument or reflecting on his writings in the hope of making a positive impact on others still appealed to him. Travel remains on his radar, but he had no interest in leisure cruises on an ocean liner or organised tours. He was wired for adrenaline-pumping activities, such as walking the Camino, exploring exotic palaces, and performing random acts of kindness, which suited his natural disposition. Upon closer analysis, he shifted his focus to relationships, spiritual peace, and quality of life. He wished for meaningful connections with loved ones, to seek comfort and freedom from pain, and to prioritise maintaining independence for as long as possible. More than anything else, he did not want any regrets to loom large in his latter years; more than anything else, peace of mind was his ultimate goal.

The old man was contemplating deeply his reason for walking another camino. He considered how the way we live each day shapes how we'll be remembered. By being mindful of our actions, words, and intentions towards others, we can ensure that the story others tell about us will be one of positivity, love, and kindness. So a legacy of books or songs or worldly achievements means nothing at the end of our days. Does it really matter if we are remembered at all? Well, the thought passed his lips, "It is a holy and wholesome thing to pray for the dead that they may be loosed from their sin." To be remembered as someone kind, compassionate, and who helps others, you actually have to be kind, compassionate, and help others. In his contemplation, he was mindful of setting aside his ego notions and doing good, which was motivational, whether he would be remembered for it or not. Taking the time to reflect on his life and, pending death at some predetermined time in the future, may unknowingly be the reasons why he was still writing books, for his own soul's sake and that of those who might read his words, a pathway toward self-understanding and a happier, more fulfilling life.

He understood that he didn't need to fear death because it's an unavoidable, natural part of life beyond human control. Focusing on death might stop him from living fully in the present. Philosophers like <u>Epicurus</u> argue that death can't harm you since it's the end of your existence, and many religions and spiritual beliefs offer comfort by suggesting continued existence or a meaningful transition after death. So, confess our character flaws in daily wrongdoings, then forget about them. Leave them in the past with the God who has already forgotten them in the same way. Then, he told himself he needed to forget even his sorrow, even all his suffering, even his grief, even his pain.

Still, he could not help but consider how others might view him in the end. Would history remember him for his duty to others and his books as his legacy? Or would he be remembered for what he did last? Perhaps it would be what he said at the time of his death. Like Oscar Wilde was not remembered so much for his creative ability over his lifetime, but his final words, when he looked at the worn wallpaper in his room and remarked," One of us has to go."

The old man reflected for a while, his heart filled with gratitude, realising he had endured much pain, suffering, and loneliness in his life, all for his growth. Though at the time it brought him great sorrow and pain, he recognised it as the path of God's best intention. He had planned to undertake this final Camino to meditate and pray for guidance to love the rest of his years. He smiled to himself as he thought of what he might say if he died during the Camino or later, that his last words might be "Buen Camino," good journey.

Desperate plea.

A young man walks along the shore
looking for what might be
An old man climbs a mountain high
to see what he might see.

And the sailor trims his sail
into the wind
He's heading for some place
He's never been.

And the hunter tracks
a wounded animal
for the riflemen and fox
needed to heal their wounds.

And were harness
to our computer screens
escaping into movies on TV
crying out in a desperate plea.,
I want to love
let me be free
to find my heart again
let me live like a child

Holy Joe tells us not to sin
He cannot see the hearts of men
And Jesus walked the desert wide
to see what he might see.

And the sailor trims his sail
into the wind
He's heading for somewhere
He's never been

And the young man lives his dream
 The old man is content to be
The hunter and for lick their wounds
And the sailor returns home from the sea.

A young man walks along the shore
looking for what might be
An old man climbs a mountain high
to see what he might see.

And were harnessed
to our computer screens
escaping into movies on TV
crying out in a desperate plea
I want to live, let me be free

CHAPTER 10

THE AFTERLIFE

The main message of this chapter centres on the old man's wish to do one last Camino, his "last hurrah" before he leaves this mortal coil for good. Now, the author needs to be honest and stop trying to make sense of it all. For the old man in this story, as you might have guessed, is the author himself — me.

So, I will write this in the first person, emphasising the recall of hallucinatory experiences, actual events, and imaginary beliefs that have, until now, influenced what I consider to be faithful to my destiny for the rest of my life, and beyond.

For I cannot accept that life ends at death any more than I can imagine space itself coming to a halt. I hasten to suggest that my upbringing in the Catholic faith as a child influences my belief in the resurrection of Christ, just as it does for you, dear reader. Some do not believe in any form of divine being as a guiding light to the beyond and may see my current age as an attempt at living spirituality, rather than a genuine pursuit. It is not for me to convince anyone else of what I consider spiritual inner guidance to get through the day. It is to the facts of belief and faith throughout early life and my latter years that I wish to draw your attention, which may shed some light and benefit to belief in a Higher Power as a guiding light, for it is not out of fear of death now, nor to convince you of your destiny, but of insight into the afterlife as I see from past experiences as guidance for me in putting pen to paper to reinforce my ideals, goals and actions for the present and foreseeable future.

Nothing I write here can convince you of life after death. It is through my own experiences in life—marked by pain, suffering, and serendipitous events—that I draw my conclusions. It is up to you to utilise this 'knowledge' to improve your own lot as a spiritual essence towards the day, like every man and woman, you face that final curtain, for we all must not forget that we come from the dust and until dust we will return.

Some readers might give up on reading this chapter now, preferring to stay in the world with a devil-may-care attitude of 'live, laugh, eat, drink and be merry for tomorrow we die.' However, I urge you to consider what I am writing here. For myself, I have learnt that I no longer fit the world's mould, as I live in the world now, but I am not of it. This may seem like the ramblings of an old man, and to some degree, it possibly is. For I have lived most of my life according to the standards of the world, and despite my pretence, drudgery, and broken dreams, only little trinkets remain for my pleasure.

It's not that I deny the existence of Christ, of whom I have been indoctrinated, but rather that in my depressed state of mind, filled with pain and suffering, I briefly lost my way and let go of my belief in his divinity. I was without Christ for a time, and in my own shallow way, I tried my best to fill my life with pleasures of the flesh and worldly distractions. At one point, I had to prove to myself the existence of Christ on earth logically and linearly. I came to believe that Christ did walk the earth, lived, died, was buried, and was resurrected to eternal life as a guiding light for humanity to follow. I, for a time, reasoned that I could not prove Christ's resurrection, but I could believe through my creative imagination—not by my logical, linear, half-brained notions, but in a Christ of the manifest. Over time, I conclude that just as I have a right and left brain, the harmony of both gives me reason to be discerning in faith to believe in a deserted Christ. I prefer not to dwell on this too much, like in the Trinity of Father, Son, and Holy Spirit, which I was conditioned to accept. Moreover, the Holy Spirit of Christ lives within me, and as a result, I have come to believe in spirituality more deeply than I did in my earlier beliefs, and this continues to guide me. Although I must admit that I miss the symbolism and signs of my former belief, I seek guidance in silence, without necessarily praying with words.

There is more documented evidence, in the Bible and other credible recorded literature, that confirms the reality of the Christ on earth story. Myth or reality, modern-day people are either believers or disbelievers. A living Christ is an internal thing; I have come to accept this as a belief. Whether Christ appears in the Roman form, as the Christ in the biblical account that calms traditional believers' minds, or as a Christ of one's own imagination, is not the concern. The dead Christ can only, in my view, be a Christ of imagination, of an inner consciousness- a manifestation, whatever realm one chooses to follow.

We view Jesus through 2,000 years of history, and he appears among the greats. Indeed, he is among the greats, but the immediate experience of his life belongs to a minor school or movement that was largely ignored and mostly unknown. Consequently, it is unlikely that there will be a significant revival of contemporary recognition of his life and times. What we can expect is that second- and third-generation historians will mention him in light of a new and rising movement that claims him as the faithful Caesar (the Lord, Saviour, and the Son of God). Ancient historians and those not-so-ancient scholars asked: Who was this Jesus, and who were his followers? Later historians are aware of the emerging movement and share whatever information they can gather about its founder. The details are humble. They concern the followers who called him 'The Christ.' His relationship to another teacher named John the Baptist, who was beheaded for his beliefs, and his followers were poor and ignorant. There were lies and rumours spread about Jesus. This is what we find in Josephus, Tacitus, Suetonius, the letter of Pliny the Younger, and others such as Lucian and Samosata, to name a few of the many. So, why then does the idea that Jesus never lived persist and gain popular assent? The answer is a simple fact, as mentioned earlier: there is no contemporary witness to the historical Jesus. The earliest we can go is Paul, an educated Roman soldier, who stated that Jesus was once a historical figure (2 Cor 5:16) and knew 'the brother of the Lord' (Gal 1:19). Still, it remains true that no eyewitness account of any incident in Christ's life has ever been found. This fact often underpins the belief that Jesus was only a myth.

The second reason supporting the idea that Jesus was a myth is because this belief is partly correct. Much about Jesus is indeed myth. In fact, much about anyone, including ourselves, is mythical. With Jesus, as with Confucius or other ancient teachers about whom little is known, myth comes as part of the package. The earliest Christian movement did interpret Jesus in light of Jewish scripture, especially the prophets. The dying and rising of Jesus fits with the idea of divine figures in pagan gods, as well as biblical references where the concept of regeneration is common. Jesus' death and resurrection match these universal mythical patterns perfectly. Early educated Christians could rely on both Jewish and Greek, as well as later Roman, sources for this. Thirdly, it's a simple fact that many early Christian preachers spoke in Jesus' name, saying things he never actually said. Christianity gathered a collection of Jesus' sayings that included both historical and non-historical inspired statements about Jesus' nature, his divinity, and the realm of the Kingdom of God. While the commentary on the parables uses parables, it is not just that.

There isn't much a historian can do about this situation except understand it. Still, this doesn't prove that Jesus never existed. We all want something to believe in, and sometimes, when we're unsure, our reaction is to discard the whole thing. I felt this way in the year when my entire world seemed to come apart. I believed many things about my life from childhood to adulthood that turned out to be myths. It all seemed to unravel in one year, when my life went pear-shaped. In that year, I lived for and believed in something that was desecrated to dust, as it was a tragedy to befall me and mine. A wedge between the young and old took an evil hold, and I watched helplessly as the fruits of my labour, my then-perceived reason for living, withered on the vine.

It is said that wisdom comes with age. All I know is that my life experiences have brought me to a place of understanding, for better and for worse, which I now want to share with you in the hope that some inner light may shine for you as it has for me. Overthinking life often leads to frustration and a focus on trivial material possessions. The reality is that we do not honestly know ourselves, our purpose, or where we might end up on the other side—except through acceptance of what is and faith that we are on the right path. Believing that the creator of all things, the infinite intelligence I call God, has a divine plan for me, as he does for everyone in humanity, if we listen to our inner voice—or sometimes, voices.

There are many inner voices we may hear; some may be hallucinations, but those that come to us in the dead of night when we are in the twilight zone of sleep seem to be concerned with guiding us. There is a higher voice of nature, while at the same time, there are the lower voices of our base nature, whose purpose appears to be of no genuine concern, focused on giving lewd imaginings and anti-spiritual stereotypes to lead us astray. It is the Higher Order voices that override the lower, weaker ones, just as they do in broad daylight.

We may experience the development of our soul life during boyhood, which, as it did for me, shows the acceptance of beings that live within the trees and bushland, which I came to see as natural, uncreative beings residing within my imagination. Now we understand it is part of the natural order to go deep within ourselves to appreciate music and tones that cannot be explained in earthly terms or where the muses inspire us to create something out of nothing. Paradoxically, the more we are in tune with ourselves, the more we appreciate what lies outside our understanding. However, there is a school of thought that the more aware we become of the world, the more we become aware of the supernatural.

We have evidence supporting the idea that men in the remote past had a direct sense of contact with the dead. Archaeological findings show that modern humans belong to a type known as Cro-Magnon man, who appeared on Earth roughly fifty to eighty thousand years ago [see Australian Aboriginal recorded historical artefacts illustrate this], and who seem to have wiped out their predecessors, Neanderthal man. This earlier race of mankind was still quite ape-like and probably communicated with grunts. In their graves, mysterious spherical stones are found, likely representing images of the sun, along with other ritual objects, suggesting that, like the ancient Egyptians, they believed in some form of life after death. It is hard to believe that creatures barely steps above apes could develop such an idea of an afterlife. I once considered the thought that Neanderthals were much more 'psychic' than modern humans. Their belief in life after death was less about philosophy and more about direct experience.

In his memory of life after death, the old man recounts: "When my mother died nearly ten years ago, she visited me in the twilight hours before I fell asleep one night. She appeared in the darkness of my bedroom, no more than a metre from my headrest. Mum just hovered there for a while, ghostlike but ever present, and looked at me with sad eyes. She did not speak, but I could hear her: "You're a good man now." Then, before she faded away like a mist, she said that "she was all right now living on the other side."

In my Irish heritage, I was often told that I could communicate with the dead. Even now, sometimes before I close my eyes to sleep at night, I hand over to the spirits of the past, my ancestors. And I ask my deceased closest kin to look after my departed son, who died by his own hand. This somehow eases my feelings of anxiety, and I can then sleep peacefully. From historical writings, it is clear that the living and the dead have often communicated. Such an art, apart from those who claim to be mediums, has a long history. Perhaps in prayer and meditation, mantras still occur, as many answers have come to those who trust in God's slow work in this regard. My childhood teachings always emphasised prayers for the dead as a routine practice.

The author of this book recalls: "I must not forget the wisdom of teachings that explain the spirit world is woven from the material of human thought. For thought, as it exists in man, is only a shadow picture, a phantom proof of its actual being. Just as the shadow of an object on a wall is related to the real object that casts the shadow, so is the thought that arises in man linked to the being in the spirit land that corresponds to this thought. The idea of the spirit world is somehow far more convincing and thought-provoking than accounts of life after death that make the spirit world sound like a cross between fairyland and some holiday destination."

In my experience, encounters with the dead occur when we go to sleep and again when we wake up. These times are very important for communicating with what are called the dead, as well as other spiritual beings from the higher spiritual realm. We might ask something of past spirits during these moments, coming from deep within our souls. Conversely, the moment of waking is much more suitable for communication, as it arises from our Higher nature and not from the quieter voice of our base nature or weakness. When we get an answer, it often comes from deep within our souls.

As the author of this book and not merely the old man, I must add that while I have had personal experiences with symbols and signs that have influenced my life, I will focus here on those that affected me during my first walk along the Camino de Santiago. Initially, during times of great suffering, I used to take long walks in the bushland near where I lived at the time. It was actually imaginary experiences that prepared me for real ones, setting the stage for my later visionary moments. In preparation for my last Camino journey, I encountered rocky cliffs and caves of Aboriginal significance, which I later realised were thousands of years old, where our Aboriginal ancestors had lived and camped nearby. I also came across a long staff-like pole, which I used on many walks while recovering from mental depression and anxiety. It was a long staff, much like the one Moses might have used to lead his people out of Egypt to the promised land. My staff had a long indentation from the middle to the top, which I connected to symbols of strength, determination, and resilience. At a key point in my recovery, I buried that staff near the site of my deceased son's grace, some years before I embarked on my first Camino.

One evening, after attending a group counselling session at the city hall, I picked up a medallion on the street. On the back, it was a replica of the staff I had recently buried, and on the front, it showed a man walking with two poles. Above him, a dark crow was flying away. In the foreground was a plain, with a mountain range behind it, surrounded by a flowing stream. At the base of the medallion was a small crucifix. Coincidentally, while I was deeply depressed, a black crow would often swoop down and sit nearby. I took this as a sign that it was connected to my dark mood and told it to leave, as I saw signs of evil in its eyes. Then it happened that a sage with a deep understanding of my condition interpreted a dream that seemed to support what was on the medallion.

So it was that some years later, I walked my first Camino, and I experienced the symbolism of that medallion with the walking poles, the Pyrenees Mountains in the background, the flowing streams, the depression leaving me like the black crows' departure, and a reconnection to the manifested Christ of my newfound faith. It was a metaphor of sorts, for it was on that journey that I fell into the dragon's mouth with tremors and emerged with a lotus flower of creative ideas that continue to drive me to this day. Strangely, I carried that medallion through the subsequent two Camino journeys, and on my return to Australia, I lost it somewhere along the way. Some intrepid travellers, luckily, may also discover the symbolism of the medallion in their spiritual recovery.

Throughout my life, I have encountered many guiding symbols that have shaped my journey. Some of these have been religious, such as crucifixes, rosary beads, prayer books, statues of saints, and the Virgin Mary. Those from non-Christian beliefs might see these as superstitious nonsense, but at the time, they held importance in the path I had chosen—those of spiritual guidance. In hindsight, they were images meant to lead me into prayer, reflection, and a connection to the Higher Power.

In a basic sense, I let go of my religiosity and turned to symbolism, which was more about the flesh's will- active symbolism of my need for gratification and my nature. I learnt from a bitter experience that I had long been on the wrong path. Consequently, it became necessary for me to approach God differently. To live spiritually without relying on Christian artefacts. It must be said that, although I sometimes retreat to gaze at a statue or pray for God's guidance under the crucifix's mantle, I also seek the guidance of others. I haven't felt the need to seek God's plan for my life, leaving that to His will rather than my own.

In my lifetime, I have read about and spoken to people who have experienced near-death experiences, gaining instant knowledge about the secrets of the ages, the entire meaning of the universe, the sun, the moon—everything. An all-powerful knowledge opening up before the witness. They also spoke of being told about their own mental illness, which would linger for a while before recovery. I now tell of a case of a mate who had landed on his head in a motorbike crash in his early twenties, and after being unconscious for a week, confirmed a vision of being led down a tunnel towards a bright light, and from the entrance, his own deceased father came and beckoned him to come forward. He told me later that he had said to his dad he wasn't ready to go to the other side, as he had more living to do. Immediately, he regained consciousness and lived another four decades before passing of cancer. Even then, he told me, "Why me? I am not ready to go." It seems that God and his dad had other plans for him in eternity.

Those who gain deep insight during their transition from this life to the next often recall fleeting moments that fade away once they return to earthly existence. I am now describing someone unconscious on the operating table in a hospital during World War II. He described his out-of-body experience as feeling like leaving his physical self to explore different states of existence, sometimes travelling in real-time to distant locations. While still unconscious, he remembered tracing airborne objects across vast distances over the USA at night and seeing a light in a village below. He went to a barroom, where the light was on, and observed ghost-like figures trying to enter the bodies of drinkers at the bar. Later, he described arriving at a facility where people worked inside a dome-shaped laboratory with powerful computer-like equipment. He could see a city of light in the distance, but before he had the chance to enter, he was returned to the hospital room and regained consciousness.
In the late 1950s, long after his out-of-body experience, the man was travelling by car with friends across Texas, USA, and told the driver to turn off the highway onto a dirt track, as he had a feeling that not far away was a small village. Sure

enough, they entered an old, ramshackle town from the days of the American Wild West. Here, he found the pub he had visited during his out-of-body experience. Later, on the way back to New York, he was reading the weekend newspaper, and the headlines had an article with drawings of a proposed dome-like structure that strangely housed Labourites experimenting with new computer technology. This was the very same dome he had visited during his out-of-body experience in World War II.

While all of this might seem like a figment of the imagination, I believe that the universe has many ways of conveying its message. In a sense, it wants us to 'wake up' and become aware of the cosmic dimensions of the drama we are all part of. Near-death experiences are one of the methods used to wake us up to a higher reality—one we should accept as part of living, preparing us to move on to a new eternity when our time comes.

Some claim to have had or still have connections with spirits from another world, those who receive messages from the dead by hearing the voices of long-since-dead relatives. Equally, those who encounter messages from beyond using a device known as an Ouija board, or spirit board, or a talking flat board marked with the letters of the alphabet, numbers, and the words "yes" and "no," which participants use with a sliding planchette to supposedly receive messages from the spirit world.

Some believe in a hidden Hierarchy on Earth, a mankind that reassures individuals that there is a conspiracy for good within it. Of course, this is a notion that should not be dismissed. After all, all religion is based on the idea that we live in a wholly mechanical universe, and that there is, in fact, some higher form of intelligence guiding the evolution of man. Whether man is in the process of evolving from comparative imperfection to a higher state of physical and spiritual evolution, and that the evolutionary process in all its phases is directed by high intelligences who have themselves reached this higher state. Then there is the Artificial Intelligence notion that argues purely on scientific grounds that man will make a machine behave if it has intelligence itself, that the computer programme will be able to create its own intelligence. Thus, there will be no need for man. It flies in the face of the fact that a human programmer is needed to create the program in the first place, and human intelligence is of far greater order in the hierarchy of living things than any AI can ever be. Anyway, I am getting away from the point of my story here. And I won't be here in the long run to see if such a creative endeavour comes to light. It certainly has not been the case in any of humanity's past creations to the present day, so why, you may ask, will it be so tomorrow? If the benefits of AI do not serve mankind, then why should it take over humankind?

There is much I could go on about here, from the workings of cosmic rays to the sun, moon, and stars, from beneath the ocean and beyond the deep blue abyss. From the writings of great scientific minds, philosophers, insightful geniuses, scribes, poets, and sceptics, on the mystery of what remains of life after death and what awaits us there. In fact, the reason for my current situation in my dotage, which I attest to, is interrelated with a pilgrimage in my vision for the present here on Earth, which is my calling for now.

Overlooking fear of the pending doom of not making it to Santiago, the daily sufferings of an ageing body tramping along, the acceptance of being alone with my thoughts and what fate may have in store before the final ending, the tramping of another pilgrimage of the Camino for all its foolhardiness in my twilight years is no more crazy than the idea of any belief I may have without proof of the afterlife for me. I am content with my aspirations, which require me to be faithful to my own destiny.

The Crossing

Each word is a sip of water
near the mouth of men
Silence is the sound
of meditation

All you feel is walking
all you hear
the sound of feet
You are not thirsty now

There is just a sound
like a whisper
in the wind
like ice under one's feet

You are not here yourself
moved to another world,
You are not here yourself
moved to another world.

You are at the crossing,
hear the sound of your own feet
Upon the journey
You are on The Way.

A blind man crossing new borders
He carries his knapsack
crossing the borders
of The Way.

You are not here yourself
moved to another world
You are not here yourself
moved to another world.

The noise is deafening.
Thunder and rain
You are a grain of sand
You are on a beach.

The storm is over now.
It is a new day
You were in the abyss,
But now you see The Way.

There is always light
in the darkest hour
Pilgrim's eyes are opening
The void is deafening.

You were not here yourself,
moving to another world
You are not here yourself
Moving to another world.

Just a bling man crossing new borders
He carries his knapsack
crossing the borders
 of The Way

You are not here yourself
moving to another world
You are not here yourself
moving to another world.

CHAPTER 11.

EPILOGUE

"The moving finger writes and having writ moves on: nor all the piety and wit shall lure it back more cancel half a line. Nor all thy tears wash away half a word of it." These lines from the 11th-century Persian poet Omar Khayyam speak to the irreversible nature of time and fate, suggesting that once something is written or a moment has passed, it cannot be undone, regardless of one's intelligence, regrets, or sorrow.

In writing this book, I am reminded of Omar Khayyam's words, as everything I have written is now complete. The course of this book is not exactly what I expected when I began, as it was more of an introspection of my current self in the early years of my eighth decade. Mindful of the approaching end, the importance of maintaining health, building strong social connections with family and friends, pursuing personal interests, and contributing to the community through activities such as volunteering or mentoring become a priority. In these later years, it is natural to seek fulfilment in life by focusing on positive ageing, engaging in lifelong learning, and embracing experiences to find peace and purpose, rather than dwelling on limitations.

So, while I focus a lot on past and present issues in each chapter, I still become fixated on the meaning of life again: overcoming the fear of death, letting go of the past, and living in the moment, accepting whatever outcomes come. Even more so, I see the importance of continuing creative pursuits that I had little or no chance to follow in my previous life before retirement.

So, what I have gained for my own benefit in shaping my world through thought, word, and deed, I also trust that you, the reader, gain some benefit for your life and living as well. For in sharing my strength and hopes that the reality of a spiritual existence, I trust, is your reward. Furthermore, the acknowledgement that none of us, still living life, regardless of our doubts, fears, and hopes, knows what lies beyond, suggests we should not worry too much about it. Instead, live the day in peace and harmony as best we can, for what will transpire will surely be the pathway we are meant to tread.

In my ageing body, I still have the desire to step out again and walk another Camino de Santiago. It might happen if I prepare myself for this adventure as my final long trek before I turn to dust. Age isn't the criterion, but the ability to live each day as it comes, regardless of what comes my way. I remember attending the Pilgrims' Mass at the Cathedral in Santiago at the end of my last Camino. The priest in his homily said: " You have walked your pilgrim's path through the 'dark' night of the soul and emerged at the end of your journey into the light. Now it's time to live, really live."

So it is, dear reader, that you reflect on the contents of this book, whether you are young or old, for we may cross paths along The Way someday, and I can offer my personal blessing on your life journey as I take my final leave. And if we do not meet, then I wish you happy trails in your daily life, whatever road you walk.

If you desire to know more about the Camino Way or, indeed, what My creative output has developed for me as I walk the joyful path of destiny over the past decade or so; then visit my website www.caminoway.com.au for all things Camino. If you wish to listen to an audio or read a narration of the journey, head to the "About Us" page. There, you'll find an audio and written introduction narrating The Way.

Additionally, you can view a summary of my books on my website's book page and at all online bookstores. For my songs, visit the song page to listen to some tracks from the album via the provided music links. Alternatively, head to YouTube and search for "Top Songs Doug McPhillips" to access all my albums for free.
At the risk of repeating myself, the website, the books, and the albums would never have existed without the creative inspiration that the Camino pilgrimages sparked within me. It is that journey that attracts the young to its magnetic pull, marking their transition from the spiritual to the material world. Likewise, both older individuals like me and the not-so-old walk The Way to let go of worldly burdens, seek new direction and purpose, and discover a newfound freedom that cannot be described in words alone.

Some pilgrims see the journey of the Way as a link to ley lines believed to connect historic or ancient sites, holding spiritual significance for those who walk there. Others like me are drawn in by the many mythical beliefs discovered along the Way, which undoubtedly influenced me to write three books about the Camino. There is also a connection between the Milky Way and the Camino de Santiago, both literal and symbolic, dating back to ancient Celtic beliefs and medieval legend, where the Milky Way was regarded as a "Path of Stars." Some historical accounts suggest the Milky Way was used as a navigational guide for ancient routes and inspired the name Santiago, after the apostle James. The term "Compostela," associated with the Camino, may even mean "Field of Stars."

The story of St. James, the apostle of Christ, and the pilgrimage across northern Spain, following the main routes and the Milky Way, remains alive today. It was there that he reportedly preached in the name of the crucified master that " Faith without works is dead. " He was expected to return to Jerusalem around 40 AD, where King Herod Agrippa beheaded him, and his body floated Viking-style on a barge towards Spain. The story goes that seven of his followers buried his body on a hillside where they were eventually laid to rest themselves. About 800 years later, a fisherman determined to find James's burial site followed a light appearing on a mountainside near Santiago, where he discovered his remains. The local bishop was eager to boost funds for the war against the Moors. At the time, they identified the bones as those of the Apostle, blessed them, and buried them beneath the altar at the Cathedral of Santiago.

The reported battle between the Moors and the Christians for the Iberian Peninsula—a land rich with treasures of bronze, silver, and gold—became the setting for a mythic tale of St. James's involvement. It recounts St. James riding a white steed, leading the troops into battle with a fiery sword as his guide, and of the Moors carrying a mummified arm of Mohammed as their emblem. There are no historical records of this battle, nor evidence that St. James ever set foot in Spain; he probably never rode a horse in his life, much less commanded troops. Besides Christian symbols and signs found throughout Iberia and around Santiago, many cult images—including witches—persist today despite the pilgrimages to Santiago to honour the saint.

About the Author

Doug McPhillips, poet, singer, songwriter, and author, commenced his journey of discovery over a decade ago after life-changing experiences.

The many tracks he has traversed through the Northern Hemisphere and down under in Australia and New Zealand have contributed to the facts and beliefs about the spiritual essence of this novel.

Doug has written twenty-five books, many of which relate to personal spiritual growth and belief.

Doug is an adventurer who divides his time between family and friends, his creative pursuits, and those who benefit most from his efforts and experience.